About the author

Alan Wong was born in Nuneaton Warwickshire in the United Kingdom. He graduated from The University of Central England in Birmingham in 2001 and it was during his time here that he became fascinated with Aesop's Fables; although as much as he desired to write a fable of his own the task proved too difficult. Then, twelve years after he had graduated, an old colleague communicated with him via social media about the relationship between her and her pet cat. What she said eventually led to his first fable "The Cat and its Owner" and for this reason is the very first story in his book, *Life and Soul in Fables*.

To Dawn, Sophie, Edward, Michael and Vivien. For it is they who have made this book a reality.

Alan Wong

LIFE AND SOUL IN FABLES

AUSTIN MACAULEY
PUBLISHERS LTD.

A CIP catalogue record for this title is available from the British Library.

ISBN 9781786125064   (Paperback)
ISBN 9781786125071   (Hardback)
ISBN 9781786125088   (E-Book)

www.austinmacauley.com

First Published (2016)
Austin Macauley Publishers Ltd.
25 Canada Square
Canary Wharf
London
E14 5LQ

1 - The Cat and Its Owner

There was once a simple cat whose rich owner doted on him. She bought him the best food, the best toys and everything else that a domestic cat could ever want. The cat however did not show himself to be anymore content each time his owner presented him with another gift although he also did not show himself to be discontented. Then one day the cat fell ill and the owner became concerned. She therefore stopped buying him the gifts and spent more time nurturing him, hoping he would recover. The cat, despite being in a state of ill health responded with delight seeing his owner showing this kind of affection towards him. When the cat eventually recovered he showed signs of more contentment and was very active and energetic, almost like a renewed animal. He would always seek his owner's attention and when he got it he would become very playful and happy. The owner and her cat considered each other to be family.

* * *

This fable shows a number of important aspects of life not just for people but also for animals in general.

Bonds between individuals can be made strong to the level that each would consider the other as family no matter how different they may be. It is also easy to think that such bonds between actual family members exist naturally but are in fact made in the same way. Just as champions are never born, neither are the bonds between individuals, they all have to be made.

We as people often allow our materialistic needs to consume our minds to the extent that we neglect the things that are really important to us. In the case here the owner was led to the belief that this same materialistic nature extends to her pet cat and therefore ignoring what was really important to him which was the bond they share.

2 - The Eagle and The Chameleon

An Eagle was out hunting one day. With its amazing eyesight it could spot its prey from great distances and could always strike with precision. He landed on a branch of a tree, wings outstretched before settling onto the branch and waited for his favourite prey to appear. Nearby, a Chameleon who also has great eyesight had spotted him before he arrived and immediately changed his colours to match the leaves on the branch on which he was sitting nervously.

Without even looking at the Chameleon, the Eagle spoke to him. 'Do not worry my friend. I can see where you are, for not even your sophisticated disguise can fool my eyes. But today I am in search for more worthy prey, I do not need to waste my time with you.'

'Thank you sir,' replied the Chameleon. 'For your eyesight really does stand up to what they say when you hear the phrase *an eagle's eye* but there are still things you do not see.'

'Do not insult me fool or I may change my mind today and decide that a lizard like you will be my next meal.'

'I apologise sir if I have shown disrespect but it was not my intention. For I have noticed that you always look before you and rarely behind you. Look behind you once in a while and you may find there are important things that you should take notice of. As a chameleon I know this because I can move each of my eyes in any direction I wish without the need to move any other part of my body. I have found in the past many things behind me that could have caused me harm or could have benefited me.'

'I am a bird of prey. I have no need to look at what is behind me for I have nothing to fear and what I leave behind is of no importance.'

A moment later the Eagle then spotted a large rodent on the ground and immediately readied himself for the kill. But just as he was about to take off, he felt a pain in his back and suddenly for the first time in his life, he saw nothing. He fell to his death. A hunter whom he ignored had shot him.

* * *

This fable shows that those of us who look too far ahead tend to forget what is behind them.

3 - Friendship and Wine

There was once a wine maker who spent most of his time at his winery and vineyards. His wife had passed away many years ago and he had no children. He lived a lonely but content existence; his vineyard and winery were his life now. He grew the best grapes and made the best wines in his village, a feat that he was very proud of. Every few days he would pull a cartload of grapes, wine and even carry some jars of wine into town to his customers. One day he was carrying many jars of wine on his back and was also pulling a cart full of his finest grapes and wine. He stopped for a moment to rest and put down the haversack that clung to his shoulders. After a short rest he picked up the haversack, gripped the handles of the cart and he was on his way. After travelling for a few more minutes, he again felt the strain on his back and shoulders from the weight of the haversack and his hands were beginning to feel numb from gripping the handles of the cart. He stopped suddenly as his hands could not hold on for any longer, when he looked up again he saw a man approaching him from the opposite direction who then stopped right in front of him.

The man looked at him and noticed the wine maker breathing heavily and sweating. He then looked at his cartload and the burden he carried on his shoulders. 'Good day my friend. They are some fine looking grapes you have there and the wine I recognise from my local wine vendor in town, it is one of the finest available in our village. Are you on your way there?'

'Yes sir, I have several customers there who are unable to collect from me. I therefore must deliver their orders in time to make the sale.'

'Then let me help you. It is still at least an hour's travel before you reach town and I would hate to see our village deprived of this fine wine and grapes,' said the man and then he took hold of the handles of the cart and made his way into town with the wine maker. When they reached town the man continued to help pull the wine maker's cart to all his customers until the cart was empty.

'I cannot thank you enough sir. Almost all my life I have lived through such hardship of having to carry a heavy burden but you have made this particular day an easy one. I just wish I had some way of repaying you, I wish I had brought an extra jar of wine now so I may give it to you as a gift for your kindness.'

'There is no need my friend. Like I say; your wine and grapes are the finest, just being able to sample it in our village is a gift in itself.'

'I hope I get the honour of meeting you again someday.'

The two men then clasped hands and then parted ways.

A few days later the wine maker had an even larger delivery to make and again the journey into town was demanding for him. On his way there he met the same man again who out of kindness helped him again by sharing the load and helping him deliver to his customers. When they were about to part ways the winemaker pulled out a single jar of wine from his haversack.

'This is not much of a reward for the good deeds you have done my friend but it was all I could persuade my last customer to give back to me. Please take it as a token of my gratitude,' said the wine maker

'Why thank you my friend. You say it's not much but when it's the finest wine in the village then it most certainly is. Please, my house is not far from here, I am a baker by trade. Join me for a drink and a simple meal, it would mean a lot to me if you could.'

The wine maker accepted the offer and the two of them sat together and enjoyed a meal of cheese and bread with a jar of the fine wine that the wine maker makes.

As the weeks passed the two men met each other again on numerous occasions whenever the wine maker had to make a delivery. And each time the baker would help him in his travels and out of gratitude the wine maker rewarded him with gifts of grapes and wine and each time the baker would invite the wine maker to his house for a meal and a drink. Over time the two became good friends and the baker would even go to the wine maker's vineyard at times to visit and to help in him in his work. The wine maker in turn would at times go to the baker's bakery, offering free jars of wine to his most loyal customers. Each time they met, they would share a jar of wine together at the end of the day.

* * *

This fable shows the importance of friendship. As long as friendship is made for the right reasons and is in the right place and the bonds are strong, then friendship is really just like wine itself becoming more valuable and greater as time passes.

4 - The Ant Colony

A large column of Army Ants was on the march one day, lead by their First General. As they marched in search of food to feed the colony they came across a large garden situated next to a small river, the garden was rich with plants and vegetation grown purposefully by its gardener. The gardener though welcomes the ants to his large garden because he knows that they are not interested in what he has grown or planted but the other insects that his garden attracts. The ants are here to feed and prey upon the pests that plague his garden. However, another large column of rival ants was approaching from the other side of the river. The two sides were from competing colonies and therefore would not share the loot with one another. Whatever prize that this garden has to offer would have to be fought for, and a battle between the two sides was imminent. The First General looked on over the other side of the river and saw the enemy ants approaching and beginning to build their bridges to cross. The first general called his column to a halt. His subordinate The Second General also observed the situation.

'It seems that their strength in numbers is the same as our own. We can cover the distance between our current position and the river in less than an hour sir. If we march now, then by the time we are within striking distance they will have only crossed half of their forces at the very most. We can then easily overwhelm them and take out half their troops in one quick swoop,' said The Second General.

The first general did not respond and just looked on patiently

'Shall I order the column to advance sir?'

'Yes,' said The First General.

The column of ants then began its march. By the time the column had come to within striking distance of the enemy, the opposing side of ants had only managed to transport half their numbers onto the battlefield.

'Shall I give the order to attack now sir?' asked the Second General.

'No.' replied the First General.

'Sir?' asked the Second General with concern.

'I said no general. Keep our forces where they are and I will give the order to attack.'

The First General waited with his troops patiently until the opposing side had crossed their entire column. Then he gave the order to attack. The battle that followed was long and bloody and the enemy proved to be stronger than expected and even more determined. In the end, the First General and his column were defeated and forced to retreat back to the nest. His subordinates were furious and disappointed, the Second General immediately appealed to the Queen.

'Your Majesty. I am here to inform you that the First General is incompetent; he cost us victory in a very important battle today. He showed the enemy too much respect and he values his honour more than he does the colony. You must relieve him of command and appoint me as his replacement.' The Second General pleaded.

'The First General is one of my most loyal subjects. I cannot remove him without just cause. Tell me exactly what happened today second general.' responded the Queen.

The Second General explained to the Queen what had happened and then the Queen requested a private meeting with the First General. After a long private discussion, the Queen announced that the First General would keep command of the military. His subordinates looked at him with disgust and jealousy.

The next day the First General led another column to another garden, rich with the resources they required. The garden this time was situated next to a hill but just before they could reach it, another column of enemy ants was charging towards them. It was a matter of minutes before the enemy forces would strike upon them.

'Sir if we move our column up the hill the enemy will then have to attack us there and therefore it will slow down their advance and give us a chance to charge down upon them,' said his subordinate the Third General.

'We shall hold our position here general. Be ready when I give the order to advance forward.'

'But sir, we have no advantage here,' said the Third General.

'You have your orders. Do as I say.'

The Third General obeyed. The two sides clashed with one another brutally. The battle was fought long and hard but again the First General and his troops were defeated and he was forced to order a retreat. Back at the nest, it was the Third General this time who appealed to the Queen. He explained the situation to her and again she sought a private audience with the First General and then announced to her senior subjects that the First General will retain his command.

The next day though the First General led his troops to victory over the same enemy that they met at the river the other day. He recognised the enemy's strength in their centre lines from the last battle and therefore split his entire column into two separate forces to concentrate on the enemy's left and right flanks. This allowed him to avoid the more powerful troops in the centre whilst his own troops took out the weaker enemy soldiers. Then the next day he won another great victory over the same enemy they met by the hill. This time he used their tendency to charge against them by ordering his centre flank to slowly retreat themselves during the heat of battle bringing the enemy's centre lines forward catching them in a vice between his left and right flanks. These two victories brought the colony huge spoils of war.

A few days later one of the soldier ants was curious on why the First General let victory slip by him so easily on the two battles they lost.

'Sir. You seem like a great military commander but why did you let us be so easily defeated in the past.' Asked the soldier.

'Because it was necessary for us to learn defeat,' said the First General.

The soldier did not understand and looked on like he was confused.

'You must understand my friend. If we defeat the enemy by chance today, then we still have to face them again tomorrow with the uncertainty as to whether fortune will favour us again. However, if we can defeat them on equal terms today then we can face them again tomorrow with the knowledge of their strengths and weaknesses and therefore with more certainty of victory in our own hands.'

The soldier looked at the general in awe but felt puzzled again by something else. 'But weren't you afraid of the Queen relieving you of your command?'

'No.'

'How did you know she wouldn't?'

'Because she values loyalty more than victory. When she realised what had happened when we were defeated in those two battles she admired me for my honour and honesty. Someone in her position of power will always fear being betrayed by her subjects. Whilst she saw honour and loyalty in me, she only saw ambition in the other generals.'

* * *

This fable shows two important ideals. It can often be regarded that defeat with honour can be viewed with more value than victory with dishonour.

It is also important that we must first learn how to deal with an enemy on equal terms before leaving anything to chance.

5 - The Doves, The Dragon, The Dog and The Owl

The doves are a symbol of love and they pair for life. A mating pair built a nest together and after the female laid her eggs, both parents took turns to incubate and look after them. The male dove incubated the eggs in the morning till after noon then the female took over for the rest of the day. But one evening when the male was out whilst his mate looked after the eggs, he mated with another female dove. His mate knew of this because when he returned she smelt the scent of another dove on him. The female, feeling inconsolable due her mate's unfaithfulness flew away when the male took his turn in incubating the eggs. She never returned.

The dragon is a symbol of power and wealth. There was once a dragon who was so powerful and rich that all feared and envied him. His great power and strength allowed him to defeat many of his own kind and many others, allowing him to accumulate immense wealth in gold and treasure. His fame and fortune spread throughout the known world and everyone soon came to respect and fear him. But such fame and fortune would always attract those who were hungry for power and driven by greed. Year after year, the powerful dragon was continuously challenged. It did not matter to those who challenged him that they may die, his fame and vast fortune made the temptation too strong. After defeating many challengers, the once powerful dragon became weak through injury and exhaustion and had to use his fortune to tempt others into helping him. At times he even reasoned with his enemies by giving them some of his treasure in order to maintain peace, until one day he had nothing left and was weak and vulnerable. The once rich and powerful dragon had now exhausted both his wealth and strength.

There was once a dog who was very faithful to his master and they did everything together. They adored each other's company, the dog obeyed his master's every command and the master would often spoil the dog with good food and attention. But one day the master was busy and forgot to feed the dog, when he eventually remembered, the dog ate very ravenously and whilst he did so the master went to stroke him. The dog felt threatened as he thought the master was going to take his food away from him and bit his hand. Enraged by such behaviour the master turned on the dog and banished him.

The Forest Owl was renowned for his knowledge and wisdom. One day the Squirrel asked him for advice.

'How can I make it easier for myself to gather the harvest for winter? Asked the Squirrel.

'Harvest more than you need this year and therefore you would not have to work as hard for the next year,' replied the Owl and then he paused for a moment. 'Also, if you do find that your supplies run low during the winter, the sugary residue from the bark of the sugar maple trees can also be harvested to help you through the winter.'

The Squirrel was grateful and thanked the owl for his advice.

The next day a Mole asked him what it was like to see the world.

'Everyone keeps telling me just how beautiful the world is but I am blind and I see only light and darkness,' said the Mole.

'The world is whatever one perceives it as. For some of us can see but we only tend to look at the things we want to see and nothing else beyond. Also the entirety of the world cannot just be seen because there are an abundance of things that can only be heard, smelt, tasted and touched but no one is gifted enough to fully experience it all. Although your sight is lacking and you cannot see much, nature has gifted you with an amazing sense of smell and touch. Therefore, you can catch the scent of the world better than most and there are certain smells that you can experience that others cannot. Your enhanced sense of touch also allows you to touch and feel the qualities of the earth that cannot be seen with any eye.'

The words of the Owl inspired the Mole and enabled him to understand how to use his gifted qualities to perceive how the world looks to him.

Because of his wise counsel, many other animals went to see the Owl to be inspired and for his advice due to his knowledge and wisdom. When the Owl eventually died, the animals of the forest built him a shrine and engraved upon it his most famous words. They also recorded and kept much of the advice he gave them as reference for future generations.

* * *

Few things in the world can last forever. Love can be insincere, wealth and power can be spent and friendships can end. But knowledge and wisdom will stay with us until the end of our days and even live on after us.

6 - The Wolves and The Swans

Swans and Wolves share a common social bond. They pair with their mates for life.

A swan and his mate had been together for years. She was his first mate and he was also her first. One day he had reached the end of his life and his mate was with him at his end. They shared his final moments together. Despite their grief, both he and his mate were happy to have spent much of their lives in each other's company. Having been through much together, they both realised that what they had was special and to them it had all been worth it.

Meanwhile a pair of wolves were out hunting for food for themselves and their cubs. The male spotted a lone bison in the distance and initiated his mate to follow him for the kill. They both slowly approached the bison, eyes locked on their prey. They stopped a short distance away from the bison and waited for the right moment to strike. Then, as the bison lowered its head to feed, the wolves struck. They attacked the bison on each side and each clasped its jaws into the bison's neck and then held on for their lives. The bison's strength though was immense and he swung his body to one side with such power that both wolves of were sent to the ground. Realising there was still danger, the bison continued to attack one of the wolves, charging its horns towards the female as she ran. Realising his mate was in danger the male wolf gave chase. His mate changed directions frequently and suddenly as she ran to slow the bison down, just before the bison caught her, the male wolf jumped and forced his teeth into the bison's neck again just as they came to uneven ground, forcing the bison to collapse onto him. His mate then immediately went for the fallen bison, forcing her jaws into its windpipe. Through the combination of fatigue, pain, difficulty in breathing and its heavy weight, the bison could not get back up in time to fight on and died. The male wolf though also died after being crushed by the immense weight of the bison. As he lay dying, neither he or his mate showed the emotion of grief as both understood the dangers of the hunt and the importance to find food at whatever cost for their young.

* * *

This fable shows the importance of one common goal but done in separate ways. One must live life in the way that suits them. In the case of the wolves one must know not to be too in love with life as there are things worth dying for. At the same time though, one must value one's life enough to understand what they have.

7 - The Elephant and The Lion

A Lone Elephant was travelling through the African Savannah in search of vegetation and water. Several other elephants travelled in the same direction, some in herds and some alone. The Lone Elephant was not travelling in a herd, like all adult male elephants he lived a solitary life. But he followed the herds and other elephants, travelling with them because he knew from past experience that where they were heading would eventually bring new sources of food and water. As the journey progressed other elephants joined, some joining alone and some in herds until eventually there were hundreds of them making the same journey. The journey took them several days, stopping only occasionally to graze, browse and drink from the limited supplies of food and water they found on their way.

After several days of exhausting travel, they finally reached their destination of the wide-open grasslands of The Savannah. Everywhere there were plants and vegetation of all kinds. Trees like jackal berry, umbrella thorn acacia and candelabra were scattered all over the area widely spaced enough so the canopy does not close, allowing sunlight to come through between the trees which allowed the grassland to grow. Bermuda grass and elephant grass covered the lands and river bushwillow grew along the banks of rivers. The Savannah provided rich pickings for everyone and the Lone Elephant was happy that he was here as were others. All around The

Savannah there were animals of all kinds, browsing and grazing on the rich and abundant food sources. Zebras, antelopes, rhinoceros and wildebeests grazed all over the grassland. Chacma baboons and giraffes browsed on the trees. But where there were peaceful animals feeding off the lush vegetation, there were also predators ruthlessly hunting other animals. As the Lone Elephant approached an umbrella thorn acacia tree to feed, he saw a warthog being mercilessly chased down by a pack of hungry hyenas. The bloodthirsty animals ran him down and caught him with several jaws of sharp teeth, his screams could be heard as his skin and flesh were being ripped and torn by the hyenas. Elsewhere the Lone Elephant also witnessed another hunt, a cheetah launching an ambush on a group of gazelles, picking off whichever one was closest to her. She used her speed and quick acceleration to catch up to a gazelle she had singled out but the gazelle was also swift and employed the tactic of suddenly darting left and right whenever the cheetah got close. This unbalanced the cheetah and thus slowed its pace and forced her to run for longer and work harder to regain speed, until eventually the cheetah was too tired to continue the hunt. The images of these predators stayed in the elephant's mind as he reached up with his trunk to the branches of the umbrella thorn acacia tree and began feeding on the leaves. He stood next to an adult giraffe who shared the tree with him.

'Those predators are just bullies. They attack smaller animals but they usually leave us alone,' said the Giraffe.

'I know, but I still I feel grateful to them even though it's hard to do so after witnessing what they do.' Replied the Lone Elephant as he tore down a branch from the tree.

The Giraffe looked at him with confusion and discontent. 'Why would anyone be grateful to their potential enemies? So they won't attack us directly, but if given any kind of advantage they most certainly would. I have also seen them kill several of our young because they are vulnerable.'

The Lone Elephant was wise and intelligent. He knew from his experience how important the predators were in terms of keeping food and resources in the balance. 'Food can sometimes be limited; those blood thirsty flesh eaters though help keep demand for vegetation from becoming unmaintainable. That is one of the reasons why there is enough food for individuals like you and I.'

As they both pulled more leaves off the tree there was suddenly commotion nearby. There was a loud splash and the sound of heavy hoofs pounding the ground followed. A group of thirsty wildebeests had just escaped the jaws of a Nile crocodile at a nearby river.

The Giraffe and Elephant looked on for a moment and then resumed eating again.

'I never thought of it like that. You are wise my friend, I now have new found respect for those creatures, even those ugly evil looking crocodiles there.'

The Lone Elephant and Giraffe continued to browse for most of the day and as time passed, other animals arrived to join them. When he had eaten his fill the Lone Elephant walked away to find a quiet place to rest. As he was resting, he looked around and curiously watched the activities of the other animals of The Savannah. He noticed that the lions were relatively small in numbers despite being the dominant predators. When he looked more carefully he also realised they were also the same lions he saw the last time he came here. The Lone

Elephant was puzzled; surely an efficient predator like the lion who can overcome all other predators with the exception of the crocodile would be higher in number. The Nile crocodiles who were also efficient and powerful predators lived in huge numbers. He approached a group of grazing wildebeests to see if they knew the answer.

'You encounter the lion most often here. Why is it that their numbers never seem to be significant despite their efficiency as predators and lack of competition from other carnivorous animals?' asked the Lone Elephant.

'I don't know. I am just glad there are not more of them. They continuously harass us and other herds and have killed many of my friends and family.' replied one of the wildebeest.

The Lone Elephant looked around, still feeling curious.

Another Wildebeest stopped grazing for a moment. 'If you're so curious to know then why not ask them yourself directly, who better to find out than you? I heard lions are very fearful of you elephants and don't dare attack your kind.'

'That's precisely the problem, if I approach them, they simply just run away in fear. I cannot ask them if they are not there and I cannot run as fast.'

'Then find a brave lion to talk to,' said another wildebeest, sarcastically.

The Lone Elephant ignored the last remark and decided to go to the river to drink.

The sun was finally setting and after an exhausting day travelling and browsing for food, the Lone Elephant slept. However, within an hour he was suddenly awoken by the sound of grass rustling nearby. Something was within the long grasses and was approaching towards him. He looked around and managed to pinpoint the source of the sound. Slowly, out of the long grass crawled a small lion cub, it must have strayed too far from its mother. Its inexperience showed and he came closer and closer to the elephant and at the same time made out calls to his mother. A few minutes later, an adult lioness appeared out of the grasses, she had heard the cries of her cub and immediately came but was hesitant to come any closer when she saw the Lone Elephant. The Lioness kept her distance for the moment; her cub was just a few yards from her but only a few feet from the elephant.

'Is this your child?' asked the Lone Elephant.

The lioness paused for a moment before answering. 'Yes.'

'Then come and claim him. He is of no interest to me.'

The Lioness slowly came forward and when she was close enough, lowered her head to pick up her cub, but just before she did the Elephant spoke again.

'I just want to know something,' said the Lone Elephant.

The Lioness was startled and quickly looked up at the Lone Elephant. 'What?' The Lioness paused for a moment before speaking again. 'What is it you want to know?'

'Why is there no other groups of lions here? I noticed that all the lions in this area belong to the same group.'

'Our pride are the only lions who control this space of land. It is our territory, we do not welcome other lions here, what roams these lands belong to us.'

The Lone Elephant looked at her with disdain.

'With exceptions of course,' said the Lioness and then picked up her cub and left.

The Lone Elephant watched her leave and when she was out of sight, he went back to sleep.

The next morning the Lone Elephant was on his way to a nearby river to drink again. As he got closer to the bank he saw the large body of a lion sitting on the water's edge, other animals quickly kept their distance from the Lion but the elephant had no natural fear of lions and just kept walking. When the Lion heard him coming from behind he turned around to look and what he saw quickly got him to his feet. He was about to leave but what happened next surprised him. The Lone Elephant called out to him.

'Wait. I want to ask you something,' said the Lone Elephant as he as he got closer to the bank. He made sure he kept his distance from the lion, as to not startle him, making sure he was not within striking distance. 'Why are there so few of your kind in such a vast land? You seem like a successful species, you do what you do very efficiently, it is strange there are not more of you.'

'This territory is ours; we do not share it with other lions unless they are born from our own pride. That way there is more food for us,' said the Lion.

'But the resources you control in this vast land is enough to support five times your current numbers. We elephants always share resources with each other and animals of many different kinds. That way, with the exception of the right to mate, we do not fight amongst ourselves. We help each other.'

'We are lions; we do not share with strangers. Any other lions who cross into our lands will be found and killed. Anyone who challenges me for the leadership of this pride will also be killed.'

'You sound like you're letting your vanity control too many of your decisions. It is making you arrogant and irrational.'

'You are not a lion. You would not understand,' said the Lion and then turned around and began walking away.

'Maybe not. But I do understand that pride, arrogance and greed would be the undoing of any animal, including lions like you.' replied the Lone Elephant.

The Lion heard him but just kept on walking. The Lone Elephant watched him until he walked out of sight.

A few days had passed since the Lone Elephant encountered the alpha male of the lion pride. Today he had come down to the river to drink again. As he lifted his head up from the water he could see that there were a number of Nile crocodiles on the other side, all keeping a watchful eye out for potential prey. The Lone Elephant ignored them and looked out into the distance, he could see a male lion sitting out in the open plain, but then looked more carefully and realised it was not the same lion he had met the other day. This male lion had a bigger and darker mane and seemed larger in size. The lone elephant began thinking about his encounter with the lion a few days ago. 'Why would there be a different adult male lion here.' He thought to himself.

As he stood there looking at the lion, another elephant arrived at the river and dipped his trunk into the water for a drink. As he was drinking, another elephant also arrived to drink.

'That is the new alpha male lion you're looking at there,' said the newly arrived Elephant.

The Lone Elephant looked at him. 'Really? What happened to the last alpha male?' He asked.

'I do not know, but if what I hear is true then he is either dead or banished from this area now. Lions have this strange tradition of ruling certain areas where other lions are not welcome.'

'I know,' said the Lone Elephant as he looked into the distance. He thought about the other alpha male lion he met the other day. He would never seem him again.

* * *

Whenever one competes with another, the outcome of the contest would often lead to disappointment and despair for one. But if we learn to co-exist in peace without the need to compete then we can all be content without deriding or harming one another in any way. When we feel the need to compete, it often leads to vanity and arrogance because the need to be better than the next person can make us aggressive in our thinking that we come up with ways of how to be superior or how to prevent others from becoming superior to us. This can lead to aggression, violence and disrespect towards others. Because like an addiction, this kind of attitude can grow over time and encourage us to do unpleasant things just for the sake of winning, being better than others or feeling the need for revenge when we can't succeed.

8 - The Leatherback Turtle

A baby leatherback sea turtle was struggling to get out of her shell. It was a few months since its mother had nested her, she was ready to hatch out of her egg and face the dangerous task of her journey to the sea. She struggles to break out of her egg until she feels minute grains of sand coming through the shell, she senses a crack has formed and continues to work on the area where the sand is coming in until the sand comes pouring through in a constant flow. As the shell opened she could feel the sand on her face and her instincts told her to work her flippers upwards towards the surface. As she works her way to the surface she could feel and hear all her brothers and sisters doing the same thing and they all work in unison reaching for the surface. As the sand felt lighter and easier to dig she began to see the light above. Then as she pushed aside the last layer of sand above her with her flipper, the shade provided by her flipper gave way to the brightness and warmth of the sun. The intense light shone upon her eyes, causing her to partially shut them for a moment until she found herself crawling on her belly and making her way towards the sea.

'Hurry!' Shouted one of her brothers. 'We must reach the water soon.'

'But why? What is the hurry? Shouldn't we take our time in this new and unfamiliar world?' She asked.

'You have eyes to see but you are completely blinded to the dangers that lie ahead of us. Do you not sense any of the dangers that lie ahead?' Said one of her sisters. 'We should call you Slow Flipper.'

'Quickly! Head to the water, straight ahead,' said another of her brothers as they all worked their flippers, crawling relentlessly towards the sound of the flowing water.

As they were heading towards the water, Slow Flipper saw one of her brothers ahead of her stop abruptly, being dragged away in the wrong direction. The powerful pincher of a ghost crab that had just come out of the sand had caught him. He tried persistently to free himself from the crab's grip but it was too strong. Now that she had seen one of the dangers that awaited her, her instincts told her to keep moving and do not stop as she watched her brother being torn apart by the crab. As she continued her race to the sea she could see other groups of leatherback hatchlings joining up with them, some were still coming up out of the sand. Their numbers slowly began to swell and spaces between each hatchling were slowly narrowing as more of them joined in the race to the water. This gave Slow Flipper an extra sense of security. She knew that higher numbers would make it less likely for her to suffer the same fate as her brother but just as she was thinking of this she witnessed several other hatchlings being caught and dragged away by a number of crabs on the beach. A large rock bigger than any adult leatherback turtle, covered in cracks lay ahead of them as they neared the water's edge. The edge of the rock nearest to them was buried deep into the sand at an angle causing the front edge nearest to the sea to slope upwards. The front edge also had a large point at the top, resembling a small mountain. As most of the hatchlings approached the rock, their natural instincts told them to go around it.

'Go around the rock, it would be easier and safer there,' said one of the other hatchlings.

But just as they did, something appeared out of the air and landed next to the rock and the hatchlings near it started to disappear in large numbers. Several shorebirds had spotted the hatchlings reaching for the sea and took the opportunity for an easy meal. Slow Flipper was scared to go around the rock now and she felt the need to go straight towards it instead. Several other hatchlings followed her lead, working their way up the rock's slope, Slow Flipper and many of her brothers and sisters found the surface of the rock difficult to move on. The rough and uneven surface was scratching and damaging their soft lower shells and they found themselves having to work harder as they struggled their way up. As Slow Flipper reached the top, neither she nor any of the other hatchlings would stop, their instincts simply told them to keep going now until they reach the water. Each and every one of them fell off the edge of the rock and landed on the soft sand beneath. Slow Flipper landed on her belly but many of her siblings and friends were not as fortunate. Some of the other hatchlings had landed on their backs and were unable to move, struggling to get back on their bellies. Many were being dragged away or picked up by the crabs and the birds. But this also gave Slow Flipper an opportunity to make further progress on her journey, whilst these predators were distracted by the stranded hatchlings.

'It's not far now, don't stop we are almost there,' said another hatchling.

Slow Flipper could see now that the sea was just a few minutes away. She moved in unison with hundreds of other hatchlings who surrounded her, looking ahead she could see some had moved out of formation with the main body of crawling leather shells. Then she saw other pale scaly skinned creatures with four legs and long tails rush in and grab the hatchlings that had fallen out of formation. Fast moving monitor lizards had now joined in the feeding frenzy. Slow Flipper realised now the safety in large numbers and keeping herself in line with the others. As they all reached the water's edge, the column of hatchlings became thinner and thinner but Slow Flipper kept herself in the centre of the column, offering more protection as the predators tended to attack from the outside and work their way into the column.

As hundreds of hatchlings started entering the water, Slow Flipper found herself among them; she had finally reached the water. The sea felt very different and strange to her. The smooth, cool but also warmth of the water felt like a natural touch to her skin. She found she could swim much faster than she could move on land and her flippers felt like they were made for the sea. She knew then from the feelings of surprise, natural comfort and newfound strength that her journey was just beginning.

Several years later Slow Flipper found herself making another journey. She had mated with another leatherback several days ago and her maternal instincts gave her the desire to make this strangely familiar journey. After days of travelling, Slow Flipper found herself on the edge of a beach. As she crawled out of the water the feeling of the sand felt familiar to her. She looked around the beach and saw several other things that reminded her of something but she couldn't quite remember. The shore birds, the ghost crabs and monitor lizards. Then she saw the rock where the front edge pointing towards the sea had a large point at the top, resembling a small mountain. She remembered this rock and it in turn made her remember this beach. This was the beach where she was born over seven years ago. She knew now why she was here, for this is the place where she would lay her eggs and her future children would make the same dangerous journey to the sea. Slow Flipper looked at the whole beach carefully for several minutes and tears could be seen flowing down from her eyes as her face dried. Slow Flipper then decided to turn around and leave. She decided to find another beach for her eggs.

* * *

When one sees history repeating itself for them then one can see this as fate giving them a second chance in life. If something was not done right the first time, then you should go back and do it again.

9 - The Dolphin and The Orca

The Dolphin and the Orca were displaying their acrobatic skills at sea. As both are very social animals they enjoy performing acrobatic displays as a show of skill, agility, speed and general recreation. The Dolphin asked the Orca if he would care to have a contest to see who the better or more skilful performer was.

'But who would be the judge to decide the winner?' asked the Orca.

'Well I believe the humans who travel over the waves in their boats would be the best judges. They seem like intelligent beings and not only that, they are not native to the seas and will make good unbiased judges.' replied the Dolphin.

The Orca agreed and so they practiced their routines until they could spot some boats passing nearby carrying humans who could watch and admire their skills.

When they eventually spotted a passenger ship pass by, they both started to display their acrobatic skills in and out of the water. The people aboard the ship were taken aback by their display, revelling, admiring and enjoying the unique entertainment, which they do not often see. After watching the great display of playful entertainment, the people seemed to prefer the skills of the Dolphin more than the Orca. Although both were very good in their own way, the Dolphin with his smaller size and extra agility gave the crowd much more to admire. The Orca himself could display impressive breaching and spyhopping but the Dolphin though could leap higher out of the water and looked more impressive than the Orca with his high leaps and spinning in the air. The Dolphin's tail walking also looked more skilful and impressive than the Orca's spyhopping. In the end, the Orca admitted defeat and agreed that the Dolphin was the winner. The Orca felt great disappointment in the loss but it was not the first time that he had been involved in a contest with other animals of the sea and he had lost before. He therefore had grown more accustomed to it. The Dolphin though was a prouder individual. Because like the Orca, he too had competed in the past with other dolphins and orcas over their showmanship and skill, not just in a contest but also as part of his own culture as dolphins do to impress a potential mate and to locate schools of fish. The Dolphin though had never lost in the past and was generally regarded to be the best performer by all his contemporaries.

Over time both the Orca and the Dolphin would compete again with other dolphins, orcas and porpoises alike. The Orca would occasionally win or lose but the Dolphin would just keep winning.

Then one day, the two of them would meet again whilst in a playful manner and the two greeted each other with enthusiasm.

'Hello my friend. It is good to see you again,' said the Dolphin.

'I feel the same sir; it seems like it was a long time ago since we last met. Can I ask if you are still as good and skilful in the arts as you were before?' Asked the Orca.

'I should think so. I practice and compete all the time and I never fail to impress. I have also been in many other challenges since we last had our encounter and I never lost once.'

'That's good to hear. Would you care to challenge me again?' asked the Orca.

'Why of course, I could never turn away from a challenge and I have great belief in my skill and therefore have nothing to fear.' replied the Dolphin.

And with the acceptance of the Orca's challenge the two began practicing their skills as they waited for a ship carrying enough people to judge the winner to pass.

When a ship eventually came the two of them began displaying their acrobatic aerial tricks and active water techniques. Unknown to both them though the ship passing was a tourist ship that had been out specifically on the watch for pods of dolphins. They had spent the whole day watching and admiring several pods of dolphins displaying their playful skills and the guests on board wanted to see something different. For this reason it was to their delight when they saw the Orca performing on the water. The Dolphin noticed the extra attention being given to the Orca and worked harder in his display, leaping higher than he could normally, spinning in the air as quickly and as many times as he could and over exerting himself by tail walking. However the crowd continued to admire the Orca and applauded with great intensity in seeing him perform his feats. In the end the Dolphin had to accept defeat for the first time in his life. When they parted ways the Orca felt delight in winning but in a modest way because he was familiar with both the exultation of victory and the bitterness of defeat. The Dolphin however felt greatly depressed with the loss as he had no concept of losing at all and felt disappointment to an extent that he felt he could never compete again.

* * *

Before one can learn how to win, one should first learn how to lose. This way we can then learn to accept defeat more gracefully and not let setbacks cloud our judgement.

10 - The Loveless Maiden

There was once a maiden whose only wish was to be loved. Driven by her need for affection and love she found love at an early age. Her relationship though did not last as it was later revealed that her lover never truly loved her. Distraught and overcome with anguish she longed to be loved sincerely. She soon found herself another lover and was happy again for a short while. But again her lover's love for her was not true because he had been unfaithful to her and again she was left feeling lonely and inconsolable. Then she thought she had found love again but this time her lover suddenly disappeared one day without a word.

* * *

When we rush into things or try to learn too much too soon we prevent ourselves from truly understanding what the basic fundamentals of something really means.

11 - The Monk and The Maiden

There was once a soldier who had loyally served The Emperor in The Royal Army for many years. After years of his loyal service he was finally discharged with honour. Upon leaving he reflected upon his years of service in The Royal Army and remembered all the bloodshed and violence of the many battles he had fought. The ex-soldier realised that throughout his life, most of which having been spent serving in the military has been tainted with much sin. He decided then that the only way to atone for them would be to follow the teachings of Buddha and try to cleanse himself of his past. The ex-soldier then gave away all of his personal possessions to the poor and went in search of a temple to seek refuge. After many days of searching and having to live off his instincts, he finally found a temple on top of a mountain and he made his way up to the temple's entrance. When he had reached the gates, he leaned against the wooden doors with his eyes closed and began pounding them with what little strength he had left in him until they finally opened. As he listened to the creaking sound of wood and watched the doors slowly moving inwards, the ex-soldier then fell to his hands and knees and lowered his head.

'Please my brothers. I seek only to be given a chance to atone for myself.'

The two monks at the door placed the palms of their hands together in prayer and bowed their heads to the ex-soldier as they both chanted a Buddhist Greeting and then stood aside to welcome him in. They took him to see the senior monk in charge of the temple where he explained his reasons for wanting to convert himself and become a monk. The head monk listened and accepted that the ex-soldier's intentions were good and therefore accepted him as a new member of the temple. The ex-soldier was then taken through the traditional rituals and was ordained as a monk, he was given new garments to wear and began learning the teachings of Buddha.

Over the next few years he spent his time carrying out various tasks required of him for the temple, listening to the teachings of Buddha and seeking enlightenment through prayer and meditation. Slowly he began to understand how he can cleanse himself of his past sins and also realised that some of his actions and feelings during his time serving in the military was in fact good.

One day he was out to fetch water from the local well with some of his other fellow monks. As they approached the well he noticed that a young woman was sitting nearby alone. Her face was one of sorrow and she did not speak but just sat there alone. The other monks ignored her. A few days later they returned and she was there again, the same as she was a few days ago. The next time the Ex-Soldier Monk saw her he noticed that she was crying and approached her.

'What is troubling you my child?' asked the Ex-Soldier Monk.

'It cannot be helped Dai Shi. There is no answer to my problems. What I want just cannot be found,' said the Maiden.

'It can only be found my child if you truly understand what it is. What is it that you seek?'

'I have been waiting to be loved for years. But there never seems to be a single man who understands what love is.'

'What you say holds some truth my child. But love has no boundaries; few people truly understand what it is.'

The woman held her hands to her face and began to weep again.

He continued to look at her. 'There are many kinds of love, to be able to understand them all, one would have to be quite extraordinary.'

'All I ever wanted was to love and be loved in return. Is that really too much to ask.'

'As I say my child, there are many kinds of love, Buddha's teachings have taught us this. Not every individual understands, it is possible that the people you have met just do not understand the love you understand.'

The woman stopped to think for a moment and then looked up to the monk and smiled. 'How do you know so much about love Dai Shi?'

'I've told you, the teachings of Buddha have helped me realise and understand what love is. Also, I was not always a monk, I was once a soldier serving the Emperor in the Imperial Army, I once thought as you do but my commitment to the Emperor prevented me from ever being able to find love.'

'Why did you become a monk? Didn't you ever wanted to be with anyone or at least try to share your life with someone who would make you happy?'

'Yes, for a long time I did during my service to the Emperor. But over time my life adapted to accept that such a wish would not come true. It was the only way, there was never an opportunity or any kind of intervention which allowed me to find love.'

'But you are no longer in service to the Emperor, why don't you try to find love now instead of learning the teachings of Buddha?'

'Because during my time in service to the Emperor, my hands had been stained with the blood of others. It is time for me to redeem myself for my sins.'

'You seem to understand much of what love is though, then why do you turn yourself away from it? Do you have disdain for love in any way?'

'No, not at all. I admire all those who can love or have found love because I know that love can lead to benevolence. It is the only way that we people can achieve the virtue of self-sacrifice.'

'Then why don't you try and find love yourself?'

'I have lived all my life without it now and I only know how to live without it and not with it. I only need to understand it which I do through the teachings of Buddha and also through my experience whilst serving the Emperor.'

'How did you learn what love is when you served the Emperor?'

'Because when I served the Emperor I served him out of love for my country. I saw that in many of the men who served alongside with me. You see, there are many kinds of love but they are all measured through self-sacrifice which can only be achieved through love.'

The maiden looked at the ex-soldier monk with confusion.

'When you think about the idea of self-sacrifice you envision someone who is being completely unselfish and doing something only for the benefit of somebody else and not himself or herself. In practice though such a selfless act is almost impossible because no matter what you do, there is always an element of self-gain or self-gratification involved. Like you feel you have to do a good deed because you know you will feel good about it afterwards or to prevent yourself from feeling guilty for not doing so. Almost every good deed we do, there is always something in it that benefits the individual who carries out the good deed itself. However, when you choose the path of virtue out of love, then such a notion of self-sacrifice is then possible because only through love you truly will not be thinking of yourself but for others.' The Ex-Soldier Monk then looked into the maiden's eyes as she stared at him in awe. 'I am sorry my child. But I must get back to the temple now, my brothers and superiors await my return. I hope what I said will help you in your future endeavours.' He then bowed his head slightly with the palms of his hand pressed together as he chanted a short prayer and then made his way back to the temple.

The Maiden watched him walk away, her eyes firmly fixed on him until his figure faded out of sight.

A few days later the Ex-Soldier Monk went to the well again to fetch water. As he approached the well, the maiden whom he spoke to a few days earlier was there again.

'I would like to thank you for your wise words the other day Dai Shi,' said the Maiden.

The Ex-Soldier Monk held his palms together in a prayer posture and then bowed his head and recited a brief Buddhist Prayer before looking back up and responding. 'There is no need to thank me my child. My words are simply the teachings of Buddha and my experiences through Karma.'

'It does not matter to me Dai Shi, for it was you who brought them to me and for that I am most grateful.'

'Gratitude in itself is also a virtue.'

The Maiden smiled and then looked down before speaking. 'Dai Shi, every word you speak gives out inspiration. It seems you can turn misery and sorrow into joy simply with your wise words.'

'They are not really my words my child, for most of what I say is just a reciting of what Buddha teaches us. I am happy and grateful that I can put them to use to help people like you.'

'I thank you for bringing these kind words to me, even if they are not your own.'

The Ex-Soldier Monk put his hands together again in a prayer posture and bowed his head again before reciting another brief prayer. 'I am sorry I cannot continue our conversation my child, for I must leave again. I wish you the blessing of Buddha in all your future endeavours.'

After a brief exchange of words, the two of them parted company again. Over the next few months the Maiden and the Ex-Soldier Monk met on several occasions and each time the Maiden would share with him her troubles and thoughts. The Monk would then recite brief prayers and give words of wisdom and inspiration to her to lift her spirit and each time the Maiden would come away wiser and happier.

One day the Maiden was standing by the well, waiting for the arrival of the Ex-Soldier Monk. When he eventually arrived to fetch water from the well as he often did, the Maiden approached him. The Monk noticed that she seemed more nervous and agitated today.

The Ex-Soldier Monk recited another brief Buddhist prayer as the Maiden approached and then looked up. 'Is there something troubling you today my child?'

The Maiden nodded but did not speak.

'Would you like to share your thoughts with me again? Perhaps there maybe something I can teach you to help.'

There was a long pause before either of them spoke.

'I understand if you cannot talk about it. Give your thoughts time to identify themselves more clearly, once they become clear they can then be translated into words easier.'

The Maiden was silent but when she saw that the Ex-Soldier Monk was about to leave, she suddenly spoke. 'My troubles this time are my feelings for you Dai Shi. You have been such an inspiration and a comfort to me that I now feel like a different person. A better one and most importantly a happier one. No one else in my entire life has ever made me feel this way and I feel I can only truly live if I have you by my side.'

The Monk placed his hands together and recited another brief prayer. 'For I am always by your side and everyone else's. The teachings of Buddha are not just for people like myself but for everyone, we simply help

Buddha spread his teachings to help people liberate themselves from suffering.'

The Maiden began to cry as she looked at the monk. 'That is not what I meant Dai Shi. I mean I want you to be with me and protect me not only in the ways you have shown me in the last few months but I want you to help and protect me as the one you love. Because I love you.'

The Monk recited another brief prayer. 'I am sorry. But what is required of me does not allow me to experience this kind of love.'

'Isn't love important for your religion?'

'Yes. It is very important.'

'Then why can't you have it.'

'We must understand love and what it can do. There are some kinds of love we can have but there are also other kinds that we cannot. A monk's ultimate goal is to achieve nirvana. To free ourselves from attachment and sufferings. The love you speak of leads to attachment and attachment can lead to suffering.'

'Does your religion not allowed you shed yourself of your vows and go back to living a lay life if you choose to?'

'Yes, none of us are ever forced or oppressed into keeping our vows as a monk.'

'Then why don't you give up your life as a monk and be with me? You will be doing it out of the goodness of your heart and in some ways be holding yourself true to some of Buddha's Teachings.'

The Monk recited another prayer before speaking. 'I am afraid that is something that is beyond my ability now. I cannot experience that kind of intimacy because my vow of chastity helps me to be more intimate in my thoughts. The life I have lived has been through karma and it is out of karma that I no longer understand the kind of love that you seek. Even if I do give up my vows as a monk I will not be able to give you the kind of love you need.' The Monk recited another brief prayer.

The Maiden then lowered her head and cried. She walked away from the Monk and he never saw her again after that day.

* * *

This fable shows two things.

Any individual who is capable of showing love is proof in itself that that they have some good in them.

When one has to wait too long for something, then it often leads to it not meaning much or meaning too much once one has got it.

12 - The Wise Mole and The Unicorn

One day a Mole came up to the surface in search of food. He could not find any insects in the tunnels he had built that day and decided to come up to the surface in search of nuts. Despite being almost blind, he had an amazingly developed sense of touch and with this he sensed an encouraging vibration on the ground. Something nearby had fallen from a tree and he moved himself to the direction where he sensed the fallen object and found that it was a forest nut and began to feed on it. As he was feeding he could hear a distinct sound, which he had never heard before. The voice of a maiden was singing in the forest. He had never heard anything like it before, the sound was sweet and harmonious and his instinct was to follow the sound to its source. As he neared the area where the maiden was sitting he began to pick up other vibrations of a more disturbing nature, he knew then there were others in the area close by and his acute sense of smell detected the scent of gunpowder. He then felt the movements of hooves approaching and realised then that this was a ruse to lure an animal to its death. He had many times in the past felt these vibrations; smelt the gunpowder and the situation had always ended with vibrations of the collapse of another animal and the smell of a dying creature. He then moved in the direction of where he could sense the approaching footsteps.

When he felt the presence of the other animal close by, he stopped.

'Do not go any further my friend, for what you will find in the direction you are heading will be nothing other than death. The sweet sound you hear is merely an inducement to get you in position to be killed.' The Mole warned.

The animal heard him and the Mole could feel him turning his hooves and moving away to safety.

The next day the Mole was out searching for food again until he felt the movement of another animal approaching him.

'I wish to thank you my friend for your wise counsel yesterday, for if it was not for you I am certain my life would have ended. For that I wish to grant you the gift of sight, with it you will find that your search for food will be made much easier for the rest of your life.'

'Who are you?' Asked the Mole.

'I am a unicorn of this forest and I symbolise what is pure. When you come out of your burrow tomorrow, you will see the world,' said the Unicorn and then turned and left.

The next day the Mole was digging a tunnel to the surface. As he reached his destination he could see a bright light appearing slowly before him as he removed the dirt. Small spots of light shining on his eyes slowly appeared and then got bigger and bigger, then suddenly his eyes were filled with an intense brightness that almost caused him to be blind again. He reached the surface and pulled himself out until his head was fully exposed. He looked in all directions whilst holding onto the edges of the tunnel entrance. He could not see much to begin with, his newly gifted ability to see was still adjusting to the brightness of daylight. He came out of the tunnel completely and lowered his head with his eyes closed, then he slowly opened his eyes as he raised his head. He found his vision slowly clearing as everything began to take shape and focus. At first he was amazed at what he saw. Trees as tall as the sky with far reaching branches and colourful leafs and fruit. Other animals roaming the forest happily and the bright sky and sun shining upon all. But then he saw other things, trees being felled for no real reason; spaces once occupied by beautiful trees were suddenly made empty. Other animals around were being killed for sport, the looks on their faces showing the pain of death. Other objects also littered the forest, which did not belong there. The mole then turned around and went back to his burrow. He never again returned to the surface.

* * *

This fable shows that such truth, knowledge and wisdom do not always carry the expectations of benevolence. For when one becomes wise and knowledgeable he/she will have to look at the world for what it really is and what you see may not always be good.

13 - The Lion, The Hyena and The Earthworm

The lion and hyena are two of the most advanced and successful animals of the wild. As predators they are both well adapted to their environments. The lion being the most powerful and strongest of all the predators in Africa, can overpower all competition and exercise authority over all other predators. They have the size and body strength to take down even the most powerful and dangerous prey such as the cape buffalo. The hyena, equipped with their bone breaking jaws and amazing endurance, can run down any prey at top speed for a quarter of a mile, they are the perfect embodiment of an endurance hunter. However, despite these gifts neither animal can expect an easy life.

One day a group of hyenas were hungry and were out hunting. They began trailing a herd of wildebeests, looking for a suitable target they tried to single out the young and vulnerable. After hours of careful watch, they picked out their target and lay in wait. Then, there was the charge, they grabbed the young wildebeest by the hind legs and neck, it seemed like a perfect kill but they failed to isolate their prey first. Several adult wildebeests came to the young wildebeest's aid, charging with their horns and kicking at the predators. The hunt failed and the hyenas remained hungry. Later that day they succeeded in killing a cape buffalo, but not long after they succeeded they found themselves being robbed by a group of lions.

Meanwhile the pride of lions had enjoyed a successful day. After robbing the hyenas of their kill, they had by now eaten their fill and were resting. But there was danger coming their way, another male lion has made his presence known in the area by marking his scent in the pride's territory. His intentions are to take over the pride. The current alpha male called out to warn off the intruder but his calls were ignored, he waited anxiously and the lionesses were nervous. When the two males finally confronted one another, the alpha male proved too weak and lost an eye in the conflict. He was banished from the pride that now had a new male in charge. Many of the lionesses now faced a painful dilemma, do they stay with the pride and the new alpha male or do they leave and fend for themselves without the pride's protection? If they choose to stay, then the new alpha male will not tolerate any children who were not born to him and will kill them. Or do they leave the protection and the resources of the pride to fend not only for themselves but also their cubs? One of the lionesses chose to leave, taking her cub with her.

The next day the lone lioness came across a hyena; the two looked at one another, both exhausted by the previous day's events and were in no frame of mind to fight.

'Oh why is life as difficult and unfair even for creatures as graceful and prolific as ourselves,' said the Lioness.

'It is only difficult for us because of you lions.' replied the Hyena.

'We take what we can simply because we are better than you. If you don't want that to happen then you need to become as strong as us. You do the same to us lions whenever the opportunity presents itself to you.'

The two paused for a moment.

'Your lives are difficult simply because you make it that way.' A peculiar voice called out.

The Lioness and Hyena did not know or see who had spoken and looked at each other in confusion. They then looked around to see who made that last comment and could not see any other animals around other than themselves and the Lioness's cub, who was asleep. Then they looked down to the ground and found an earthworm crawling along on the dirt. They both looked at the earthworm, bemused and curious.

'And how did you come to that conclusion my simple and slimy friend?' asked the Lioness.

'You may both be graceful and prolific animals but such characteristics make your lives more complicated. Take me for example. I am a simple worm. I may crawl in the dirt but the earth provides me with all the nourishment and resources I need. I do not need to run and search for food for long periods of time. I also do not need to worry about competing with others for food and territory because being dominant and authoritarian does not matter to me.'

The Lioness and Hyena both laughed at the earthworm.

'So you're saying that all our problems will be solved if we all be like you and crawl on the earth and feed on the dirt?' asked the Hyena.

'And also to look like nothing but a simple twig of an animal covered in slime?' asked the Lioness.

'Yes. I am sure you would feel much more happy and content if your lives were as simple as that.' replied the Earthworm.

The Lioness and Hyena laughed at The Earthworm again and left.

Over the next few months the Lioness found life without her pride too difficult to cope and could not provide enough food for her cub. Her cub eventually starved. The Hyena also found it difficult to cope as the dry season of The Savannah came and took its toll on all the animals. Food was scarce and therefore competition for it was even more intense, not only with other predators but also within his own clan. He found that there were many days in which his hunger became intolerable. The Earthworm though kept crawling on the earth, feeding off the nutrients that the dirt provided; he was well fed and lived a fulfilled life.

* * *

When we keep our lives simple we make our lives easier to cope with and are more likely to be happy and content.

14 - The Olympian

There was once a child by the name of Coroebus, he was a child just like any other, somewhat liked and disliked by other children of his time and enjoyed most of the things that children would like. He came from a working class family where he lived with just his mother who was baker by trade, a profession that she was very accomplished in. Having been brought up in his mother's bakery he had developed a love for cakes and sweet bread, he admired his mother greatly for her skill in her trade and dreamed of emulating her one day. But then, one fateful day when the child was on the beach with some of his friends, he proposed to them that they should all have a race and that anyone who beats him would be allowed to share his mother's cakes with him. They agreed that the racing line would be from the edge of the water to the edge of the beach straight opposite, the distance covered would be approximately one hundred and ninety metres. He and his friends then all lined up and got themselves ready, then the shout was given to begin and they all raced forward in an instant. The first seventy metres were very even between them all, then after one hundred metres Coroebus and two other children began to pull away from the rest. In the final twenty metres the two running level with Coroebus suddenly started to slow as fatigue began to affect them but Coroebus just kept going faster and faster until eventually he won. Coroebus raised his hands in victory and apologised to his friends that none of them will be sharing his mother's cakes with him and ran home.

When he arrived home his mother had baked him his favourite cakes but also some pineapple buns, which Coroebus liked very much. He then told his mother about the race and she felt proud of him, she then told him that for every time he wins another race she will bake these pineapple buns for him as a celebration. From that day on he would go to the beach everyday just to run and he would re-enact the race by himself.

Over the next few years Coroebus took part in many races and he would go on and win many times. His mother kept her promise and baked him his favourite pineapple buns which always thrilled the young boy. This encouraged Coroebus to keep racing and he grew to love running and racing just as much as he loved his mother and her baking which in turn made him want to excel in the sport. He soon began training to be a great runner, every day he would train very hard to keep bettering himself and eventually he grew up to become a professional athlete in running. For years he would train under the strictest of discipline and commitment and this would earn him invitations to take part in major races with the fastest sprinters the world had to offer. At first he was very successful in these major events that earned him awards, medals and the right to compete in the forthcoming Olympic Games. But then, the success suddenly stopped and he found himself struggling to avoid finishing amongst the last half. He tried training harder and made himself go on an even stricter diet, but his improvement was limited and the Olympic Games were just months away.

Then one day during one of Coroebus's training sessions, his instructors spoke to him in private. He found out then that the reason why his success had stopped was because some of his rivals were using performance-enhancing substances. They spoke to him openly and made it clear that if he wished to win again then he must do what his competitors are doing, although the choice was his. Coroebus was shocked and confused, and informed his coaches that such an act would be cheating and dishonourable. His coaches simply told him that it is not cheating if everyone else is doing the same. Coroebus then went home to think about what his instructors were telling him.

Months had now passed and the Olympics were just days away. Coroebus was making his final preparations. On the day of the final race he took his position and waited for the signal to run. Then, when he heard the signal he left his mark in an instant clearing the first few metres in a split second. When the athletes had reached the one hundred-metre mark everything was fairly even, but when they reached the one hundred and thirty metre mark the rest of the field began to leave Coroebus behind. He kept up his pace but his rivals were even faster, Coroebus tried harder and managed to gain one more place but by the end of the two hundred metres he finished second to last. After crossing the finish line he raised his hand as if in triumph, everyone wondered why he seemed so happy despite his disappointing result.

As the day grew dark, the day's events had all been completed and the Olympic Stadium was almost empty. Coroebus though had remained behind and kept running. Over and over again he re-ran the two hundred metre dash all by himself until he was too tired to run anymore. He fell to his hands and knees, breathing heavily. Then he felt a hand touch him on his back. He looked to his right and found his mother kneeling beside him.

'Did you not do what your coaches advised you?' asked his mother.

Coroebus stayed silent and shook his head.

'I am proud of you,' said his mother. 'You were the real winner here today. Did you know that the Olympics started as a religious festival in honour of the gods?'

Coroebus nodded.

'Today you ran the way the gods made you to run whilst the others tried to deceive the gods.' explained his mother. She then reached into her bag and pulled out something covered in cloth. She removed the cloth to reveal some baked pineapple buns. 'I hope you still like these.'

Coroebus smiled and began to cry. He hugged his mother tightly before taking the pineapple buns and began eating as they walked together.

'Why were you celebrating at the end of the race?' Asked his mother

Coroebus looked at his mother straight in the eye before speaking without hesitation. 'Because I love this sport.'

* * *

When we want to do something that we love, then it has to be done with the true love from the heart and not for the prestigious prize that it may bring to us. This is because such prizes should not matter to us if what we do is important enough or means enough to us. The Olympian loved the sport, if he had to cheat to achieve his goal in the sport he loved; then his love for the sport would not have been true. Just like the love in a relationship, if we feel love for someone and we want them to love us, we cannot cheat to get there because then our love would not be sincerely true as we are not willing to give everything in our ability and mind to prove that love.

15 - The Owl, The Pigeon and The Crow

The Owl, the Pigeon and the Crow were friends. They all took a vow as a mark of their friendship that they would always protect one another and share the food they find. One day the Owl caught a rat and shared it with his friends.

'I am thankful for you sharing your food with me my friend. But unfortunately this kind of food is not suitable for my diet,' said the Pigeon.

'I am sorry but me and Crow are still hungry. I am sorry I could not find something we could all enjoy,' said the Owl. He and the Crow then feasted on the rat.

The Pigeon looked on and went hungry. Later that day the Crow found a dead hedgehog on a nearby road and called out to his friends. When they both arrived the Pigeon looked at the food and then at the Owl and Crow.

'My friends, I am sorry but I cannot eat this. Just like with the previous source of food, this kind of food is not palatable for me,' said the Pigeon.

'I am sorry,' said the Crow.

'We will try to find a suitable source of food for you later,' said the Owl. Then he and the Crow began eating the carcass.

The next day the three of them were out searching for food and suddenly the Pigeon found a large bowl of millet and rice. Due to his hunger and haste the Pigeon flew straight over to the bowl and began to feed. Because he hadn't eaten the previous day he had forgotten about his friends and ate all the food to himself. When his friends finally arrived the bowl was empty and his friends this time were the ones who went hungry.

* * *

At times when the decisions of the world seem unfair, the only fair decision to make would be to ensure that each and everyone one of us is treated unfairly once in a while.

16 - The Lantern of Hope and The Lantern of Pride

It was the Lunar New Year and celebrations had been going on for days. It was now time for the Lantern Festival, which officially marks the end of the New Year Celebrations. The sky lanterns were being prepared to be released, each with a message written on them as a wish to be carried to Heaven. One lantern, a plain white one, was to carry the message, "To maintain strength and respect". But as the owner was about to write this message he felt it was too much and decided to change his message to something more realistic. He decided to write, "To always work hard and think unselfishly". The lantern next to this one though was very brightly coloured and decorated, its flame was much larger than the rest in an attempt to fly higher and it carried the message, "To forever achieve prosperity and enlighten others to do the same thus achieving eternal happiness".

"The message you carry my friend is weak. Such a message will never be noticed in heaven. Your flame is also weak; it will not be enough to carry you and your message high enough. Also I am the most beautiful looking lantern. I am sure to be recognised amongst all others." gestured The Brightly Coloured Lantern.

"It is not right to ask for too much my friend, for there are even limitations on how much Heaven can give. And sometimes standing out from the rest is not always a good thing." replied The Plain White Lantern.

"Only time will tell my friend, we shall see who can reach the heavens first. It is said whichever lantern reaches the greatest height will carry the wish that will be granted."

"You are right. Let us concentrate on that."

Then the lanterns were all released and began to rise up into the air. Shortly after release though, the wind began to blow slightly harder. The Brightly Coloured Lantern caught fire and began to fall; its larger flame had caught the sides. It fell into a lake and was lost, but the others all kept rising until the distance covered their appearance.

* * *

When one's pride is too strong, one's expectations would often be too high. When this happens we would often find that our goals are too high to reach.

17 - The Ticking Clock and The Iris Flower

There was a florist shop that sold flowers of all kinds. The shop was relatively small, with a capacity to hold no more than ten people. The entrance to the store was in the right corner situated right next to a large glass window that covered most of the front so people could see all the flowers on display. A display stand stood a few feet in front of the entrance placed against the wall and another was in the centre of the store, holding buckets containing a variety of flowers. Small tables and stands covered the rest of the floor space, spread out from each other by a few feet. Everywhere you look in the store you could see assortments of roses, tulips, lilies, begonias, bessera elegans and pansy violas. At the front of the store on a small table on the left side of the large window was a single purple Iris flower placed in a glass vase. She stood there elegantly in the sunlight, radiating her beautiful colours whenever the day was bright. Her three petals looked brighter and stood out from the rest of the store every time the sun was shining. Right next to her in the left corner of the store stood a tall oak long case clock, ticking every second and chiming every hour of the day, the sounds echoing throughout the store.

'That wretched clock always ticks. I can't stand it anymore,' said one of the Roses.

'Can't that old thing do anything else other than make such annoying sounds?' asked the Lilies.

'Does he not realise by now that his sounds are not appreciated in here. Someone should shut him down for good.' complained the Tulips.

The long case clock was use to the verbal mistreatment from the flowers, he had been in the store for many years and each day was always the same. The same complaints and cruel words from the flowers never stopped, he did of course wish he could stop ticking and chiming but such a feat could not be achieved unless he was shut down. He wished that the owner of the store would shut him down or move him away but to no avail. Today was no different than any other, his continuous ticking and chiming was accompanied by the vocal complaints and criticism from the other residents of the store, and by the end of the day almost every flower in the store had either complained or criticised and condemned him for his ways. However, he noticed that the Iris flower next to him remained quiet, of all the flowers; she was the only one who had not said anything to him. He looked at her with curiosity and confusion but then with fascination as he realised how much she stood out from the rest. Not only was she quiet but also she was unusually beautiful.

'Why do you remain so silent?' asked the Clock.

There was a long silence.

'The constantly annoying noise you make has made her speechless,' said the Pansy Violas.

The Long Case Clock did not respond and just carried on ticking. Then a few minutes later he began to chime, it was now six o'clock and the store was closing. The owner cleared up the store and started throwing out some of the flowers that were past their expiry dates.

Some of the flowers in the store became nervous and fearful that it would be their turn today to meet their end. The Iris flower though was left by the window. The owner then turned off the lights and closed the store; the store was now almost completely silent, only the ticking of the clock could be heard within the darkness.

It was almost seven o'clock now and the store was still silent.

'I am sorry for ignoring you earlier, but I was trying to make use of the little time I have left,' said the Iris.

The long case clock was startled. At first he did not know who was talking to him but then he realised that the voice was not familiar to him and turned his attention to the Iris flower. 'It's all right, it was probably best not to speak when everyone else is so emotional and in full voice.' He stopped to think for a moment. 'What did you mean by the little time you have left?' He asked.

'I am an iris flower; once I have been cut from the stem I do not live for long after that. I am afraid I do not have long to live now. That is why I must make the most of the time that I still have.'

'How long do you have?'

'Three, maybe four days. Six days at the very most, then I will wither away and die.'

'But I can see that you seem to accept it better than most. Do you not fear death like others do?'

'Fear should only be felt if it can make a difference to you. But for me in these circumstances, no amount of fear can change what will inevitably happen.'

'You are wise, I admire your understanding of life and death. What is it that you wish for? What do you want in the time you have left to you?'

'My only wish for the remainder my days is to spend as much time experiencing the only joy I can.' There was then a moment of silence. 'I wish to spend as much time as I can basking in the radiance and warmth of the sun. Her nourishment is the only pleasure and joy I can feel. I want to be able to spend the last hours of my life inside the light of her presence.'

'It is a noble reason to live. I sincerely hope you live long enough to enjoy the company of the sun for as long as you can. And I hope that fate would be kind enough to give you a favourable hour when death finally comes, so that your last moments will be the sight and warmth of the sun's rays.'

'Thank you sir.'

The shop remained silent for the rest of the night with the exception of the ticking and chiming of the Clock echoing throughout the room.

The next day was the same, the Iris flower just stood quietly in her vase, taking in and absorbing the nourishment of the sun. The other flowers in the shop continued in their tirade against the Long Case Clock and he could not do anything other than ignore them and carry on ticking by the second and chiming by the hour. By nightfall everyone in the store was again silent with only the ticking of the Clock filling the air with sound.

'How are you feeling today?' asked the Clock.

'A bit weaker than yesterday. I have not long left now.' replied the Iris.

The Clock looked at the Iris and tried to deduce what he could do for her.

The next day the Iris began to look gaunt, its petals began to swivel and her colour becoming paler. The Long Case Clock looked on in despair as the other flowers kept up their ill treatment of him. By night the Iris flower was too weak to talk, the long case clock looked at her and then looked out the window into the moonlit sky. He kept his eyes on the sky all through the night and waited and waited. Until eventually the sun began to rise, he watched carefully as the light brought on by the sun grew brighter and brighter until no more light could fill the air and the Iris flower was entirely covered in the sun's light.

'Hear me my dear friend,' said the Clock to the Iris flower. Time is now on your side for I have stopped it to give you all the time you need. Now the daylight will not pass until you pass on.'

The Iris flower heard what was said to her but was too weak to respond. After that she could hear nothing else, not even the ticking and chiming of the Clock, which had always been there before. The room was now silent, nothing and no one made a sound or movement, like life had stopped and paused, time was frozen for everyone except for the Iris. She just simply stood in the sunlight and absorbed and enjoyed the nourishment of the sun's life giving rays. For each passing hour for the Iris, she grew weaker and weaker and her body continued to deteriorate. Until eventually, she died and swivelled away into dust. Then, time resumed and everyone everywhere suddenly came to life again and the Clock continued to tick.

'Where has the Iris gone?' Asked the Bessera Elegans.

'I don't know. She was there a moment ago and now she has gone. There is nothing but dust there now, it's as if she had disappeared and turned to dust,' said one of the Lilies.

Everyone in the shop looked on in confusion to the corner of the room where the Iris once stood but all they could see was an empty vase with dust on it and around it.

The Long Case Clock also looked to where the Iris once stood. 'Good bye and thank you,' he said.

* * *

If we do not respect the time, then we often forget what time we have left. Many individuals see time as an enemy that eventually catches up with them but when you respect it, it can also act as an important companion.

18 - The Tortoise and The Hare

The hare was the fastest running animal in the forest. Their champion 'Fleet Footer' was the fastest of them all. He was well admired by his own kind as well as by the other animals of the forest. All who had challenged him in the past to a foot race had been humiliated and made to look worthless, none had ever come close to beating him for he was simply too fast. However, his success and reputation had also made him arrogant and disrespectful towards other animals of the forest. Even some of the other hares of the forest had grown displeased with his attitude towards them. One day the hares all gathered in a remote area of the forest to feast with each other.

'I am fast. Too fast for any of the likes of you,' said Fleet Footer. 'I am not naturally gifted. I am gifted beyond nature. I am even faster than all the other hares of the forest. I am one of a kind. I am divine.'

'Of course you are. We do not need to hear it every day,' said another Hare.

'He has won every race against anyone who dared to challenge him. And he did it easily with very little effort. Anyone who can achieve such a feat deserves to boast.' replied a third Hare. A few of the other hares began to cheer their champion, a few seconds later the vast majority of the rest then followed and did the same. The others however, were angry and annoyed and walked away.

Meanwhile, in another part of the forest an old Tortoise was out foraging for food. He was well known to the other animals of the forest because of his age and kind-hearted nature. Some say that he was over a hundred years old. The Tortoise had lived a long and contented life, although he made no significant achievements in his lifetime with the exception of his age, many still thought that his understanding of life was inspiring and felt that he was wise. Today he had found himself a bush with some fresh leaves and began feeding; as the Tortoise was feeding he heard several footsteps approaching. He turned his head to his left and found a group of hares approaching him.

'Good day my friends. What brings you here to this part of the forest?' asked the Tortoise.

'To get away from our own kind,' said one of the Hares.

The Tortoise looked at him with bewilderment.

'It is our so-called champion, Fleet Footer. He is so obsessed with himself and his achievements that he forgets all respect for anyone else. We are fed up with him.'

The Tortoise looked at the hares for a moment before speaking again. 'Tolerance my friend is a virtue. Believe me, throughout the years of my long life I have seen many misdeeds and the one you talk about now requires tolerance.'

'We agree but the real problem is how long to we have to keep tolerating this. For we are only mortal, mere mortals like us can only tolerate so much.'

The Tortoise thought to himself for a while. 'If one can get him to stop boasting, would that be considered a great virtue?'

The hares all jumped slightly at the suggestion. 'Why of course. If you know Fleet Footer as we do then you would agree. And believe me, we are not the only ones he disrespects, almost everyone else in the forest has had enough of his arrogance and condescension.' One of them said.

The Tortoise was silent for a moment and then thought back to a previous experience. 'Yes I know. I have met your champion on many occasions. I once had the unfortunate opportunity to witness him trip over a squirrel just to takes his nuts. The poor fellow was made to run half the forest chasing your champion to get them back, only to be told to respect the champion for his athleticism and speed. I was told Fleet Footer then dropped the squirrel's nuts on the floor before him as he was panting and struggling for breath.'

'It seems you have seen the worse of him even more than we have my friend. You should understand our dilemma better than anyone else can,' said one of the hares.

'Then come back here tomorrow my friends. I will devise a plan to help you and everyone else teach your champion a valuable lesson.'

'Really? Well thank you... We look forward to hearing what you have in mind. But do you really think you can teach him a lesson?'

'Not right now no. But like everything else, it will take time. I promise by tomorrow afternoon I would have devised a plan. Do not worry my friends, I may be old and slow but that is precisely why I can think this through. My long years of experience and caution in this world has taught me that everything takes time and as long as I have it then whatever I need will eventually come to me.'

The hares thanked the Tortoise again and agreed to meet him the next day. The Tortoise spent the entire day thinking over his plans. He had to think hard about what he was about to do and whether it was worth his while in doing it. In the end he decided that he had lived long enough in peace and tranquillity, which he considered was a gift to him from the world and it was time for him to give something back.

The next day the group of hares and the Tortoise met at the same spot in the forest. The hares were anxious to hear what the Tortoise's plans were.

'Good morning my friends. Thank you for coming,' said the Old Tortoise.

'It's all right sir. There is nothing for us to lose by being here and we are really interested in what you're planning to do,' said one of the hares.

'Ah yes. My plans. I need you to convince your champion to accept my challenge to him for a race.'

The hares all stared at him in disbelief and then started to look at each other. 'But sir, what will that solve? I mean no disrespect but your plan is folly, there is no way you can beat him in a foot race, nobody can.'

'There are more ways to win a foot race than just being fast. Just have him agree to race me and I believe that he will have learnt his lesson once the race is over.'

'I do not know what you hope to achieve here my friend but if you expect him to feel compassion or remorse for you when you finally cross that line then you are gravely mistaken. Like we said before Fleet Footer has no regards for anyone other than himself, his arrogance and selfishness is even greater than his speed in running.'

'It does not matter. Just do me this favour by arranging this race and your problems will be solved. Besides, what have any of you have to lose?'

The hares all thought for a moment until one of them looked at the Tortoise again before speaking. 'There is nothing for us to lose my friend but what about you? If you go through with this, you will be the subject of ridicule and could spend the rest of your life under the condescension and mistreatment of Fleet Footer.'

'Believe me, it will not matter once the race is over. I am old my friends and I do not have much time left in me to make a significant contribution to the world. Would you please have this arranged for me?'

There was a moment of silence until one of the hares reluctantly spoke. 'As you wish sir. We will arrange this race for you and get back to you later with the details. We wish you all the luck that fate can bestow upon you. But please, are you sure you want this to happen?'

'Yes my friend and thank you for your help and concern. I will look forward to seeing you all again later.'

The hares then went back to their part of the forest to inform their champion of the challenge put forward by the Tortoise. When Fleet Footer heard the news there was a roar of laughter amongst the hares.

'Is this some kind of joke my friends? Because if it is then you are all champions of mischief and humour,' said Fleet Footer.

There was a brief silence. 'No... this is not a joke. The Tortoise really has challenged the Great Fleet Footer to a foot race.' replied one of the other hares.

There was another moment of silence. 'You're really serious? That Tortoise who can barely make it out of his house in time for breakfast before the sun goes down has really made this challenge?'

'Yes.'

'Go back and tell him not to waste my time. I would probably die of boredom having to wait for him to get to the starting line.'

'But sir, if you refuse wouldn't that make you look unfavourable in front of the other animals of the forest. Think about it, the great champion of the hares backs down at the challenge from a tortoise.'

Fleet footer stopped and thought for a while.

'And even if it is not worth your while in taking up the challenge, you could use this opportunity to set an example to others. Like the difference between confidence and sheer foolishness, something that each one of us needs to learn. When that Old Tortoise crosses the line, I am sure he would be in no condition to even speak. You can use this notion in your victory speech and mock the old animal for his delusion.' explained one of the other hares.

'Not only will it set an example but it will also show that our champion is not just a champion of athleticism but also of true wisdom.' Another hare suggested.

Fleet Footer thought deeper until a large grin slowly appeared on his face. 'I like the way you think my friends. Yes, this would be a good opportunity for me to raise my status further. Very well. Organise the race for tomorrow. No actually make it three days' time. I want to make sure that Tortoise has enough time to show up,' said Fleet Footer before he burst out in laughter again. The rest of the hares all laughed along with him, although the few who were on the side of the Tortoise laughed unenthusiastically.

'The race will be in three days' time. It will start just outside the forest on the southern side and end by the river just a mile into the forest. The racing line has been made as straight as possible to make things simple,' said the Hare.

'Thank you. I will see you at the race in three days' time.' replied the Tortoise.

'Are you sure you want to go through with this?'

'I know you still have doubts about the wisdom of this race but like I said before, all will be revealed favourably for us once the race is over.'

'Well it is your choice my friend but some of my fellow hares and I have been thinking. As much we hate Fleet Footer for his arrogance and disrespect it does not justify you having to be humiliated like this just to try and help us. The race itself will also exhaust you my friend, you do not deserve to suffer like that.'

'I am touched by your concern and I thank you for it. But it will be fine. I will see you in three days.' replied the Tortoise and then made his way home.

The hare watched him leave and felt in awe of his bravery and determination.

On the day of the race Fleet Footer and few of the forest animals were waiting at the starting line for the Tortoise to arrive.

'How much longer do we have to wait for him?' Asked Fleet Footer, feeling irritated. 'We have been waiting for hours now. Maybe I should have given him more time,' he chuckled.

After waiting for another hour the animals at the starting line saw the faint appearance of the Tortoise coming out of the forest. After another thirty minutes he had reached the starting line already breathing heavily from what seemed to be a great exertion from him.

Fleet Footer stared at him as he waited for the Tortoise to catch his breath. 'It's nice of you to finally show up old man. Shall we begin?'

'Of course and may I take this opportunity to thank you for accepting my challenge. I know I am not much of a challenger for your great ability so it is an honour to be able to race with you.'

Fleet Footer laughed. 'Believe me old man. This is not a challenge. It is more of a life lesson that I plan to teach you.'

'Nevertheless, I thank you for it. However, I am surprised with the small turnout, where is everyone?'

'Most of them are at the finish line near the river. They await my imminent arrival.'

'I hope they will still be there when I arrive.'

'Oh they will be. I will make sure of that.'

After a brief discussion of the rules a Fox declared the race will begin when the leaf he drops hits the ground. He walked up to the starting line and stood next to Fleet Footer and the Old Tortoise as they both waited anxiously. The Fox waited a few seconds and then dropped the leaf. Both Fleet Footer and the Old Tortoise watched as it floated down. Fleet Footer disappeared off the line the moment the leaf hit the ground but the Tortoise though needed a few seconds to turn his head to the direction he was going and then slowly made his way off the line, taking another few seconds before his entire body crossed the starting line. The Hare made quick progress and reached the finish line in just a few minutes. All the animals of the forest greeted him with a loud cheer when he crossed the line. The Tortoise though had not even covered a few metres in that time and they all waited patiently for him to finish. After three hours one of the hares that supported the Tortoise went to check his progress. When he eventually saw him, roughly just over half distance of the race he noticed the Tortoise was exhausted from his efforts.

'Come my friend, there is no need to go on any further, you have already proven more than what is expected of you to have come this far.' The Hare pleaded with him.

The Tortoise was breathing heavily and was barely able to speak. 'No. I have come this far now and it is pointless turning back,' he said as he struggled on.

'But you cannot exert yourself any further, it is no good for you. Your body and your age may not sustain it.'

'That maybe true but because of my age I must finish this race. I have lived this long peacefully and happily. I must make a contribution to the world no matter how small.'

The Hare realised that there was nothing he could say or do to convince the Tortoise to give up on his cause and went back to the finishing line. The Hare explained to everyone what he saw and of the Tortoise's determination.

'It has been over four hours now, why does he keep going? It sounds like this race itself could even take his life.' asked a Fox.

The Hare thought for a moment before speaking. 'He is actually trying to help us. We discussed with him about how fed up some of us are of Fleet Footer's arrogance and disrespect for the other animals of the forest. And he felt that he could solve this problem by challenging him to a race. I do not know why or how.'

The Fox looked at Fleet Footer who was chatting and laughing with his friends about the Tortoise's slowness and how they were to embarrass him when he arrives. Then he ran off to meet with the Tortoise. He saw the Tortoise trudging along slowly, each step he took seemed to take longer than the last, the Tortoise looked like he was about to collapse. When he saw the Fox approaching he stopped for a moment to catch his breath.

The cunning Fox looked at him in the eye. 'I know what you are trying to do my friend but it will not work. You are hoping to win the admiration and sympathy of the crowd when you cross that line but the champion hare has other plans. I can see that he has prepared a victory speech to ridicule you. Its best if you give up and go home.'

The Tortoise started to think to himself for a moment and then he slowly started moving again. 'Whatever he has to say in his victory speech will not bother me when I get to the finish line. Just go back my friend and I will see you there.'

The Fox stood and stared at the Tortoise as he slowly moved passed him and then ran back to the finish line to inform the other animals of what happened.

'That old fool is so stupid that he even spurns good advice.' laughed Fleet Footer.

One of the hares supporting the Tortoise was starting to feel concerned and asked the Fox what should be done.

'I will speak to my good friend the Owl. He is wise and far sighted maybe he will know what to do.'

The Fox explained the situation to the Wise Owl and how some of them are concerned for the Tortoise because the race was over exerting him. The Owl immediately saw what was going on and flew to meet with the Tortoise. When he saw him on the ground he landed next to him and began reasoning with him.

'I know what you are trying to do my valiant friend. But is it really worth what you're willing to give?' asked the Owl.

'Of course it is… I am old now… and what I can achieve today… will make my long life worth living,' said the Tortoise whilst he was still pushing himself exhaustingly forward and struggling with each word.

'But don't you have anything else to live for?'

'Of course… but I have already lived for everything else. Today's purpose… requires something… else from me.'

The Owl could see what the Tortoise was doing and knew that he had made up his mind and will not change it. He then flew back to the finish line.

It had been almost five hours since the race started, everyone waited silently until they saw the faint figure of the Tortoise slowly making his way to the finish line. The forest animals began talking amongst themselves.

Fleet Footer grinned as he watched the Tortoise approaching. He was thinking about the speech he would give once the Tortoise crossed the line. After another forty-five minutes the Tortoise finally arrived and crossed the line to finish the race. He struggled with each step, taking several deep breaths after each and then he stopped completely and looked around himself to see all the animals of the forest staring at him in silence. As he turned his head to face directly forward he saw the feet of none other than Fleet Footer himself, standing over him about to make a speech. Then, out of sheer exhaustion the Tortoise collapsed, he slowly lowered his head for the last time and his eyes slowly closed. He was dead and everyone looked on in shock.

The Fox came forward and stopped by The Tortoise's body. 'Tortoise has shown us today what real heroes are and has died for a good cause. He should be commended and immortalised for this day.' shouted the Fox.

Fleet Footer was shocked by the comment. 'No! He was nothing but an old fool who didn't know when to quit!' he shouted at the Fox. 'He died out of foolishness.'

'No he didn't,' said the Owl as he flew down and landed next to the Fox. 'He died trying to help others. You may not realise this for your ego has always got in the way of your thoughts. Almost every animal in the forest is completely fed up of your arrogance and condescension. Tortoise here felt compassion and sympathy for all those whom you've humiliated in the past and that is why he challenged you today.'

'What challenge? He never stood a chance, whatever help he planned to give to you, wasn't much if anything. It took him over five hours to complete a one-mile race. If I was him, I wouldn't even have bothered.'

'Of course you wouldn't! You are just a selfish individual who only thinks of himself. One who wants more than what he can give. You only race others to boast and condescend them and because you know you can easily win. It does not take much of an effort for you to win a race let alone finish one. But Tortoise here gave his life just to help the rest of us. That is something greater than what you would ever be able to achieve. He has given us his life. What have you given so far?

Nothing but arrogance and disrespect.' explained the Owl.

'Now who agrees with me? Tortoise should be immortalised and have a shrine built dedicated to him to commemorate this day!' shouted the Fox. The crowd then roared and cheered after hearing his words.

Fleet Footer could not refute what the Wise Owl said and stayed silent as the crowd cheered. Some of the animals even pushed themselves past him to get to the Tortoise's body so they could carry him to a safe location to be buried.

* * *

It is often a virtue to give more than you take but it is also an even greater virtue to give more than you have. When we accomplish something significant, the achievement itself would not mean much if one did not have to try very hard to get there.

*Note: This fable is in no way disapproving or an attempt to better the original classic by Aesop. It is simply an alternate version of how I feel the story could have gone.

19 - The Nile Crocodiles

A large group of Nile crocodiles were hunting at the river. They all waited patiently in the water, waiting for suitable prey to come within range for the ambush. At times they could end up waiting for days or even weeks for an opportunity but today an opportunity had presented itself early. Their ears had picked up a low frequency sound of a distant stampede and it was coming towards the river. A herd of wildebeests were heading in the direction of the river in their search for water and the crocodiles waited with their unrelenting patience. The sound of the approaching herd was getting louder and clearer by the hour and as the hours passed, the crocodiles continued to listen out for sounds that could tell them that the moment they have been waiting for is here. Within minutes the loud trampling sounds of hoofs came roaring towards to the river. Wildebeests began appearing out of the bushes and trees and started to align themselves all across the edge of the river in desperation for water. The crocodiles looked towards the herd with their eyes just above the surface of the water and then submerged themselves underwater and quietly swam towards the water's edge. For several minutes the wildebeests seemed to be drinking peacefully. Then suddenly, a large splash of water came rising up out of the water, the huge jaws of the crocodile came shooting out of the river, wide open with its sharp conical teeth exposed and then snapped shut in an instant. The first attempt by the crocodiles had failed but seconds later another attempt was made further down river and this time the jaws of the crocodile had shut firmly under the neck of one of the wildebeest. Soon, there were wildebeests falling one after the other all across the river bank and being dragged under the water and drowned. The feeding frenzy would soon begin.

The afternoon had gone well for the Nile crocodiles, each successful kill drew more crocodiles to the kill site helping to rip and tear up the carcasses before they were consumed. While this is being done, feeding is first given priority to the larger and older crocodiles. This was the way of the Nile crocodile, although they do share food and resources, there is strict code of conduct between them in that they have a strict hierarchical society. The largest crocodiles can feed first, but occasionally this code is broken.

A young and confident crocodile had been watching the afternoon hunt; he was hungry and had only had some fish to ease his hunger, a minor consolation. He wanted a proper meal. He had not yet taken part in a kill and had not even helped in taking apart a carcass but confidently swam towards a feeding site. He was aware of the Nile crocodile's code of conduct but did not care, he wanted to feed and he did not see why he had to give priority to anyone else. He saw a large older crocodile feeding on a large carcass and moved in to feed himself ignoring the fact that an older and bigger crocodile was still feeding. As far as he was concerned, he was his equal despite having done nothing to justify that. The reaction though was hostile and the older larger crocodile attacked him viciously but the young crocodile would not yield and the fight went on. The fight was quick and bloody, resulting in the young crocodile losing one of his fore legs. Bleeding and hungry the young crocodile left empty handed.

The next day, the young crocodile was still hungry, having not fed himself properly since the incident the previous day. The injury he sustained was hindering him from hunting successfully. In desperation, he tried to take first priority in the feeding again only to be attacked by a larger and stronger crocodile who responded violently. The young crocodile tried to yield this time but it was no use, he suffered another serious injury and died later that day.

* * *

Although subordination may seem like humiliation at times, we must also realise that it is also a symbol of respect. One who can accept their place with dignity is less likely to show the characteristics of arrogance and selfishness and therefore keep themselves out of harm's way.

20 - The Wandering Dog

A Dog was wandering through the wilderness alone and homeless. For the last few years of his life he had been without a home because his last owner had died in a fire leaving him with nothing and no one to turn to. He lived off the scraps left behind by wild animals and any food he could get from anyone who would take pity on him. His experience and instincts told him to keep moving on in search for better prospects. When his last owner died he tried staying where his last home was in the hope that he would see his owner again or that someone else would take him in, but there was nothing.

One day the Dog was wandering through the forest. He was hungry and with nowhere to go but after searching for what seemed like an eternity, he caught the scent of something that he had not smelt for a long time. It was a scent that he has not come across since he last had a home, the smell of roasting meat. The smell was intoxicating and alluring and he followed where his nose and hunger took him. He found himself approaching a man crouching near a fire with what looked like a roasting pheasant, just a short distance away from the fire were the carcasses of some other pheasants. The Dog sat a fair distance away from the man, a trick he had learnt in the past to ensure that others know of his non-confrontational intentions. When the man spotted him, the Dog stayed where he was, kept his eyes on the man himself and then slowly bowed his head down as an act of submission. The man looked at the dog fondly and smiled, he tore off a piece of meat from the roasting pheasant and then approached the dog. He crouched down just a few metres away holding out the piece of meat. The Dog slowly approached and gently took the meat from his hand. The man patted the dog on the head and they then both sat together eating by the fire. The Dog felt happy and contented that he had found someone kind enough to show him compassion and the man was happy for the company the Dog offered.

During the night as they slept by the fire, the Dog suddenly awoke, something within the bushes has alerted his senses. He kept quiet, listening carefully to each and every sound but all he could hear was the crackling of the fire. Then suddenly, there was a rustling in the bushes, the dog immediately stood right next to the sleeping man and began barking. The man awoke to find the dog barking towards the bushes, he looked in the same direction but could not see anything out of the ordinary but his senses told him to arm himself so he quickly grabbed his spear. They both waited patiently, looking into the darkness to see if they could spot anything, then suddenly the Dog turned around and found a wolf leaping out of the bushes. The wolf had been lured here from the smell of the pheasant carcasses and it tried to grab one of them. The Dog instinctively confronted the wolf and the two of them were entangled together biting and scratching in a violent embrace. The man did not know how to react; he could not attack because both the Dog and the wolf were struggling close together, moving violently. He quickly picked up a torch and lit it with the fire. He pointed the flaming torch towards the wolf and Dog close enough to separate them, the wolf looked at him growling viciously, the Dog stood by the man's side barking at the wolf. The man picked up one of the pheasant carcasses and threw it as far as he could over the wolf causing the animal to turn and run after it.

The man had a look at the Dog's wounds and tried his best to bandage them; he took him to a healer of animals the very next day to have his wounds checked and the Dog soon recovered. The man eventually decided to keep the Dog; he had a farm and found the dog to be very useful in alerting him when unwanted intruders such as wolves or foxes came. He also took the Dog with him on hunting trips and the Dog would help him to track down game. They both enjoyed each other's company and the Dog was happy. He had finally found a home.

* * *

If you can give someone a home, you also give them a sense of belonging and purpose.

21 - The Wandering Lion and the Gazelle

A Lion had just come of age and like all male lions who reach maturity was forced out of his pride. He spent the next few years wandering endlessly through the Savannah alone and homeless. To begin with he found his new life difficult because before he was forced away from his family, he had always depended on his pride's elders to provide food for him and had the protection of his father. But now, he had only himself to do that and it took time for him to learn. At first, he lived like a scavenging vulture, living off the scraps left behind by other animals and always retreating or finding safety in the trees whenever threatened by other predators. But with time and practice he managed to learn how to fight and defend himself by observing other animals including ones of his own kind and through the many encounters he had with hyenas and other lions. He also learnt how to become an efficient hunter, at first he only tried charging and chasing down potential prey, an idea he got from pure instinct, which proved inefficient. But then he remembered how the females of his old pride use to hunt and realised that his chances of a successful kill would be to lie in wait and ambush his prey. However, despite being able to overcome these difficult life lessons there was one problem that he could never cope with or overcome; loneliness. He longed for the companionship of other lions but all other lions he had met were all hostile towards him. He had more than once challenged other male lions for control and the right to rule a pride, but each time he failed in his attempt. Over time, he found that the grief of being alone hurt him even more than physical pain and hunger.

One day during the afternoon the Wandering Lion was resting on a large rock. He tended to move and turn in his sleep and unintentionally rolled off the rock and fell into some bushes. When he got up to move he found that he could not go very far because his tail had become trapped in the bush. He kept trying but the harder he tried the more painful his tail became, after a while he became tired again and decided to lie down and go back to sleep.

Whilst the Lion was still asleep, a young and inexperienced Thompson's gazelle approached him, the Gazelle was very hungry and began chewing and eating away at the bush where the Wandering Lion's tail had become stuck. Then the Lion awoke and saw The Gazelle eating away at the bush and he noticed that his tail had become unstuck. He got back up and this startled the Gazelle who then quickly turned and ran away to safety. The Lion just watched the Gazelle run and when it was at a safe distance away from him the Gazelle stopped and looked back at the Lion. The Lion wondered why the Gazelle would risk his life in helping him and the Gazelle himself was equally confused as to why the Lion did not try to chase and kill him like most lions tended to do. After staring at each other for a few minutes a group of hyenas suddenly attacked the Gazelle, he had become too pre-occupied to notice that a group of hyenas were quietly setting up an ambush for him. He managed to make a quick getaway but the hyenas gave chase and were relentless, they chased him continuously until eventually he tired and could not run any further. One of the hyenas took hold of his right hind leg stopping him in his tracks, then another clasped his powerful jaws onto the back of his neck and taking him down in the process. But then suddenly, the hyenas let go and they all ran as if in great fear, the Gazelle was surprised and confused but then looked up and saw the large face and mane of the Wandering Lion. He was fearful of the Lion but something told him that this lion was different.

'Why did you help me?' asked the Lion.

'Help you? What do you mean?' replied the Gazelle.

'Back there, you helped free my tail from the bushes. Weren't you afraid that I was going to harm you?'

'Yes, but I was hungry. Sometimes hunger drives you to do irrational things, today I nearly paid for that with my life.'

The Lion stared at the Gazelle for a moment. 'Nonetheless, you still helped me and I thank you for that.'

'And thank you for saving my life,' said the Gazelle nervously. 'I will be on my way.'

The Wandering Lion kept his gaze on the Gazelle. 'Wait!'

The Gazelle turned abruptly to face the Lion, he felt nervous and was getting ready to flee. 'What?'

'Where are you going?'

'I am going to find a suitable place for me to graze.'

'Would you like company?'

The Gazelle felt even more fearful. He felt he needed to choose his words cautiously. 'Not really.'

'You don't have to be afraid; if I wanted to kill you then don't you think I would have done that by now? Or waited for those hyenas to finish you off and then steal their catch afterwards?'

The Gazelle thought for a moment and felt the Lion may be speaking sincerely. For he did not chase him when he first saw him, and he did not let the hyenas kill him or try to take advantage of the situation when they all fled. 'But why would you want a gazelle for company?'

'A lion's life can be a lonely one; it is not easy to socialise with our own kind unless you can prove yourself to be strong and powerful enough to control a pride. Besides, as you can see I am a capable hunter. If I get hungry I can find other prey, I will not hurt you. And if you run into trouble with any more hyenas or other predators I can protect you.'

The Gazelle thought deep and hard, he knew he was making a very important decision and what the Lion was proposing was not something he could expect to be offered again should he refuse. 'Your offer is interesting. It benefits both of us; it is unusual and unexpected.' The two of them stared at each in silence for several moments before the Gazelle spoke again. 'And I would like to accept.'

So from that day the Lion and Gazelle became friends and roamed the Savannah together. The Lion was happy because he finally had a companion and did not have to be lonely anymore. The Gazelle was also very good at finding water and where there was water there was also prey for the Lion. The Gazelle was nervous and unsure to begin with but over time, the Lion saved him on many occasions from predators like hyenas and leopards, something which helped him to learn to trust the Lion. They kept each other company in their travels and helped each other in whichever way they could.

One day the Gazelle went to the river to drink whilst the Wandering Lion went out to search for food. The Lion then spotted another male lion and some lionesses leaving a carcass behind, he watched and waited for them to disappear so he could then take the carcass for himself. But as he watched them leave, he noticed that the male lion was walking with a limp and from the look on his face he could tell that he had sustained an injury. The Wandering Lion felt a surge of excitement and determination, for this was finally his chance to be a part of a pride again and with his opponent visibly injured and disadvantaged, it was probably his best chance to succeed in his long-time dream.

The Wandering Lion began by marking his scent over the nearby trees and bushes and waited for the alpha male's response. He slowly approached the pride, calling out to the alpha male, making his presence and his intention to challenge him known. The alpha male of the pride began calling out warnings, letting his presence be known and that he would fight to retain his pride. The Wandering Lion though ignored him and continued to approach, slowly the distance between them became shorter and shorter, then, when the distance was no more than a few metres the Wandering Lion charged after the alpha male. The two clashed and the injured alpha male was the first to be struck. Injured by the initial attack and already suffering from a wound to one of his forelegs, the alpha male fell and was helpless, all the Wandering Lion had to do now was to inflict the finishing blow. But just as he was about to do this he heard his friend the Gazelle crying out for help, he also heard the sound of hyenas and knew that his friend was being attacked. He was now in a dilemma, does fulfil his dream of finally becoming part of a new pride again or does he leave and help his friend. He stopped and thought to himself as the alpha male lay there helpless in front of him but he could still hear the cries for help from his friend. As much as he wanted a pride and territory of his own he just couldn't leave his friend to die. He turned tail and ran back to the river where he last saw the Gazelle.

He found his friend by the river where he left him, pinned down by three bloodthirsty hyenas. He leaped onto the back of one of the hyenas and hauled him away from his friend, after realising what had happened the hyena fled. The other two hyenas then let go of the gazelle and tried to attack the wandering lion, but he caught one of them in the neck and snapped it with his powerful jaw. Seeing his companion dead before him the last hyena quickly turned away and ran. The Gazelle got back up after the hyenas had left. He was wounded as well but not seriously.

'Are you all right?' Asked the Lion as he was trying to catch his breath.

'Yes. Thank you for saving me again. Are you injured as well?' asked the Gazelle.

'No. Just tired.'

The Gazelle looked at his friend with gratitude but also with guilt but he did not know why he felt guilty. 'Lie down. Rest. I will keep an eye out for any further trouble.'

The Lion lay down and rested. He was too tired to go back and challenge the alpha male of the pride he had encountered earlier. He also later discovered that the pride had already been taken over by another male lion.

* * *

This fable shows two things:

Even individuals of very different natures can learn to be friends if they can learn to understand one another. And it takes a much stronger and braver individual to be able to give up victory and accept defeat for a greater cause than it does for an individual to achieve a thousand victories.

22 - The Raven, The Crow and The Wise Owl

The Raven, Crow and Owl were friends and one day the three of them agreed to meet in the forest to socialise and talk about their unique individual attributes. First to arrive was the Raven. He was a large and intimidating figure, twenty-seven inches in length, a large black beak, a wingspan of forty-six inches and a deep croaking voice. Many other animals in the forest would cower from him due to his fear inducing characteristics. He sat on branch, waiting for his friends to arrive and a few minutes later the Crow came darting down and landed next to him. The Crow looked similar in appearance to the raven but she was much smaller and less intimidating and she also did not have his deep croaking voice. But what she lacked in size and intimidation she made up for with her ravenous and hard-hearted appetite, she would eat almost anything and did not care where the food came from.

'Good day to you,' said the Crow.

'Nice of you to arrive so soon. Now where is our old friend Owl?' asked the Raven.

'I don't know, I have not seen the old man for days, I hope he makes it, it would not be the same if we all could not be here.'

After talking to each other for several minutes they then saw the Owl slowly drift towards them and land on the branch. The Owl was very different to his two companions. He was very light in colour and his beak was a different shape. He was slightly bigger than The Crow but not as large as the Raven and tended to speak slower and quieter than his two friends.

'It's good to see you both. How long has it been since the three of us got together like this?' asked the Owl.

'Too long!' laughed the Raven.

'The better, for now we are happier than ever to be here.' remarked the Crow.

'So what have you both been doing since the last time we all sat together and talked?' asked the Owl.

'The usual. Every day is a struggle to survive so I spend most of my time looking for food. Thankfully, for me this forest offers a variety of food and there are always rich pickings. Just yesterday I managed to poach six eggs from a nest I found in the trees. Oh they were tasty just as eggs usually are,' said the Crow.

'I amuse myself by exposing the weak and pathetic in this forest. Just my presence is enough to scare and intimidate most animals. I find it most amusing when I see the look of shock on their faces or how fast they turn tail.' Boasted the Raven. 'So how about you my friend, you have so far remained quiet.' The Raven asked the Owl.

'I do the same as you both but in moderation. Of course I need to eat as well but not more than necessary and I am a bit more particular in where I get my food. I sometimes try intimidate others as well but only when necessary, like defending my home for example.'

'You should try and live a little better my friend. There is much that the world has to offer and life is not long enough for you to sample everything so you must sample as much as you can.' explained the Crow.

'Crow is right. You should stay in the spirit of things and have a good time. Time is precious, you never know just how much of it you have left,' said the Raven.

'Yes you are both right but at the same time you are both wrong. Yes, no one's life is ever long enough to see or do everything that the world has to offer and you my friend Raven, are right in that no one can be certain on how much time is left for each of us. But these are the very reasons why I should not waste too much time indulging in our basic desires such as amusement and tasting every kind of good food there is.'

A roar of laughter from the Raven and the Crow followed. The two of them found the way the Owl spoke unusual to the extreme because they knew of no one else who speaks in this way. They found such a characteristic amusing and could not hold back their amusement.

'What is more important than good food?' asked the Crow as he continued to laugh.

'And what is more important than keeping others in their place so they fear you and respect you?' laughed the Raven.

The Owl looked on with a straight face, he could see many faults in the attitudes of his two friends but he would not say anything in response.

'This is why I enjoy our conversations so much Owl and this is why we value you so much as a friend.' laughed the Crow.

'I could not have put it any better myself. Just how boring would these conversations be without you Owl, you are extraordinary, truly,' said the Raven.

'You are my friends, I aim to please you,' said the Owl.

The three of them carried on talking to one another over the next few hours. During that time the Raven and Crow both kept trying to bring up subjects that they felt would entice the Owl into refuting them and when he did, they took great joy in the laughter that it brought it with it.

'Well it has been a pleasure seeing you both again but I am afraid nature calls and needs must be met. I think I will raid another nest tonight and see if I can find some live young to feed off too. I heard there are some nests among the trees near the river, they contain some rather sizeable eggs. I also heard that they are rarely raided and therefore should be rich pickings,' said the Crow.

'I'm afraid I have to agree with you my friend,' said the Raven to the Crow. 'As good as this conversation is, I must find other ways of amusing myself. I think I will go and scare some pigeons and then I will see if I can even intimidate a human. I heard they are a challenge and that many animals of the forest fear them. Such a feat would give me much status as a fearsome animal.' boasted the Raven.

The Owl was both disgusted and worried about his friends because of the way they live their lives but he decided it was best not to say anything to them. 'Well, I look forward to our next meeting.'

'And me, when shall we all meet again?' asked the Crow.

'Let's all see each other again in six days, right here in this same spot. It can become our meeting area.' suggested the Raven.

Both the Crow and the Owl agreed with the Raven's proposition and then went their separate ways.

The next day the Crow found a nest of chicks. She had heard them screaming and quickly flew over to gather the new food source she had stumbled upon. She looked down onto the nest and found four chicks all screaming with their mouths open and coming towards her believing that she was their returning mother. But just as she was about to snatch one of them she felt a heavy and sharp blow to the face and then backed away from the nest in mid-air. She found herself being confronted by an eagle with its sharp talons spread like she was ready to grab and crush any object. She knew how powerful those talons were because she had just been caught by them and quickly took flight to safety whilst bleeding and in pain.

Later that evening the Raven saw a wooden cabin in the forest and noticed one of the windows was lit up so he decided to investigate. He sat on branch just by the window and looked inside. He noticed there was a human child sitting on the bed; she did not seem to notice him by the window so he kept staring. Then the child began to look his way but because it was now dark she could not see clearly. She got up and came closer to the window where she could see the large bird sitting on a tree branch just outside her room. The child's eyes and mouth widened in a look of fear. The Raven looked on with amusement and then opened his large beak and let out a loud croaking sound to intimidate the child further. The child screamed in terror and just seconds later the Raven saw a large figure of a man come to the child with an object in his hand, The Raven did not recognise it. Then the man took aim and the next thing the Raven saw was smoke, and the window before him smashing to shreds accompanied by a loud and deafening noise. The shot missed and he immediately took flight, the loud and destructive sound that came out of the weapon the man was holding was enough to warn him that he was in grave danger.

A few days later the three friends all met up at the same spot they shared in the forest six days ago. First to arrive was the Owl, he sat on the branch of a tree, looking calm and content with himself. An hour later the Raven arrived looking shocked as if something terrifying had happened. He just sat on a nearby branch in silence.

'You are quieter than normal my friend. What has happened?' asked the Owl.

'I nearly lost my life in the most terrifying way the other night and I have yet to recover from the experience.' replied the Raven.

Before the Owl could speak again the Crow suddenly arrived and sat herself on separate branch to the Owl and Raven. Her friends noticed a visible scar on her face.

'What happened to your face?' asked the Owl.

'I was confronted by an eagle the other day and was attacked,' said the Crow.

The Owl looked at the Crow. He was fairly certain on how she crossed paths with an eagle but decided to ask her anyway. 'But why?'

'I tried to raid a nest, it happened to be that of an eagle's'

'And how about you Raven? You seem different as well.' asked the Owl.

'I found a cabin in the forest and I tried to intimidate a child there. A man then tried to shoot me with a powerful weapon, it almost killed me.'

'I see,' said the Owl. 'I knew this was going to happen. Humans can be very dangerous my friend. For generations my ancestors have witnessed them wipe out entire species of animals in this forest, they have very destructive tools that make them particularly dangerous. And raiding nests, yes. There is always a danger to that as well, those nests that you spoke of my friend Crow, the ones among the trees near the river. That is where the eagles tend to build their nests. That is why they are rarely raided because of the dangers that eagles pose. There are many other dangerous creatures in the forest and humans and eagles are only two of them.'

The Raven and the Crow both stared at the Owl.

'Then why did you not tell us this six days ago?' Asked the Crow.

'Yes, we both could have been killed,' said the Raven.

'I could have told you six days ago. But would either of you have believed me? Both of you were so sure of yourselves that you seemed like you didn't want to believe anything else.' Explained the Owl.

The Raven and the Crow stayed silent.

'I also wanted to tell you that to raid one's nest for food is also wrong, there is plenty more game in the forest to sustain you, so why take the lives of innocents just to feed your over indulgent needs. And why put fear into people just for the sake of amusement. Only now do you realise the error of your deeds because you have done them and you have seen the dangers. Now you can learn why it must not be done in the first place even when there is no danger to you.'

The Raven and the Crow understood what The Owl was saying. Even if the Owl had warned them of the deeds they were to carry out, they would not have taken him seriously and would have gone ahead and done it anyway.

* * *

Sometimes it is better to let certain individuals commit their wrongs as it is the only way for them to understand the error of their ways. For some of us do not realise that what we are doing is wrong until we have done it.

23 - The Soldier and The Barbarian Horde

A village was informed of an imminent attack being made on a neighbouring city by a barbarian horde. The King therefore ordered all able-bodied men to be called to arms and to meet the main army at the chosen battlefield where they would confront the enemy. A local Soldier heard the news and quickly went to his barracks to ready himself for battle. When he got there he checked his armour to make sure it was in good condition and when he was content that it was, he quickly put it on and made sure that every segment was tied on tight and secured. He then picked up his sword, shield, spear and daggers and took them to the local blacksmith and asked him to make whatever repairs were necessary to perfect and strengthen them for the upcoming battle. When this was done he then gathered everything else he needed into his haversack and marched with his comrades to the battlefield to meet the enemy.

When they reached their destination the Soldier stood in line with all his comrades, some of whom were his life-long friends whom he had known since childhood. They all stood in formation, silently waiting for the inevitable. Then the silence was starting to slowly break, slow sounds of numerous footsteps and hooves trampling the ground were approaching them, and the general called them to attention and gave the order to be ready. Then the sounds slowly grew louder and faster and a cloud of dust was building up in the distance, the soldier could see the approaching enemy coming towards them. The sounds kept getting louder and the dust cloud bigger by the minute. Then, when the enemy front lines became visible to the naked eye, the order was given to charge and everyone rushed forward with their spears and swords in the air. The clash of troops was fast and hard and many who stood on the frontline fell to their deaths instantly. The Soldier caught his first victim in the throat with the tip of his spear and forced the barbarian soldier to the ground with the shaft, as he pressed the spearhead deeper a powerful sword slash came towards his chest, he caught the blow on his spear shaft, snapping it in half before he raised his shield in time to block the blade. The soldier reached for his sword and turned to face his next opponent, the moment the sword was drawn, he thrust it straight forward towards the enemy's chest, piercing flesh and bone. As the enemy soldier fell, another sword blow came swirling towards his face from his left side, he managed to raise his shield in time to meet the blow and then parry the enemy's sword away with his own. He fought on and all the time he could hear the screams and cries of dying men, the roars of battle lust and sounds of metal clashing with metal and wood.

The battle raged on all day and the tide of the battle slowly turned in favour of the enemy. As the Soldier looked around the battlefield he could see several of his comrades falling and dying. The spaces between each section of his side slowly increasing over time, groups of soldiers were being increasingly isolated from the main body of the army until they were cut down. The Soldier kept looking around himself between every few blows and clashes and saw the number of his comrades decreasing. He realised as the hours passed that there were no other soldiers on the same side as him other than the one who still stood by his side. He and his only comrade left were now completely surrounded until his comrade was caught in the neck with an arrow and he too fell. The Soldier fought on bravely until his sword shattered and a heavy axe blow knocked his shield away from him.

The fighting suddenly stopped for a moment as he reached down to his waist and pulled out the two daggers he was carrying. The Soldier looked around him and saw all the barbarians staring, laughing and mocking him. He lunged forward with his daggers striking at a nearby enemy's face but missed, another enemy soldier nearby pushed him down from behind. The Soldier fell to the ground dropping one of his daggers. He reached out to retrieve it but was met with an enemy spearhead thrusting through his hand. The Soldier screamed in agony and threw his other dagger towards the barbarian's face, slashing his left cheek, the barbarian soldier let go of the spear and let out a screech of pain simultaneously. The Soldier freed himself from the spearhead in his hand and stood up to continue the fight. He caught one enemy soldier in the face with a hard strike of his fist but then he himself felt a sharp blow to the back of his head and almost fell. He was then attacked again from behind, he felt the powerful blow of a sword slash colliding with his right shoulder, denting the armour.

The Soldier kept trying to fight on despite the combination of pain, fatigue and blood loss. The barbarians all looked at him with amusement. They shouted abuse at him and laughed like he was the subject of a joke, each time he attacked, they easily evaded him and then pushed him back down to the ground, kicking him while he was down. The Soldier then stood up for the final time. He stood there as still as a statue, staring into the eyes of the enemy who continued to laugh and mock him but this time he did not try to fight. He just stood there bleeding and dying, waiting for the end to come. Then there was silence; the barbarians stopped their taunting and abuse as their chief came forward.

'Let this one go. He is no threat to us now and he is no longer of any amusement either. He is not worth killing,' said the Chief.

After hearing their chief's words, the barbarians then started to leave the battlefield. After a while the Soldier was alone, the only one left standing alive.

* * *

Everyone has a type of strength in them that they do not know they have until it is all they have left. In this fable the best weapon that the Soldier had against his enemies all along was simply his courage and strength of character.

24 - The Atheist and Faith

There was once a soldier who was an atheist because he despised religion of all kinds. He had fought in many wars and had won battle after battle. His achievements on the battlefield just reinforced his assertions that there is no god and that life's destiny is in the hands of those who control it on Earth. One day the city was called to arms once again because they were expecting an imminent attack. Every soldier and every man who could hold and wield a sword was ordered to report to their nearest army post. The men were informed of the imminent attack and were ordered to pack all their necessary tools and belongings for the upcoming battle, and then to meet at the relevant assembly points outside of the city walls in a few days. On the night before the troops were to assemble the Atheist Soldier and his companions feasted together at the local inn.

'So how do you think this battle will go?' asked one of his companions.

'The same as always, it will be a victory but a costly one.' replied the Atheist Soldier.

'You never think that the outcome would be any different?' asked another of his companions.

'I do believe the outcome can be different but so far we have faced the same kind of enemy over and over again. Ones who are not much better than barbarians and do not know how to fight a real battle but are never short of strength and bravery.'

'I pray to the gods you are right,' said another of his companions.

'There is no need, you will find out in a few days. Besides, your gods don't often grant favours.'

'You sound like a blasphemer. You must be braver than most of us if you're willing to show an attitude like that at a time like this.' Laughed one of his companions.

'That is precisely one of the problems with religion isn't it? It strikes fear into people when they feel their faith is weak. It's better to free yourself of it and let your fate be decided in your own hands.'

His friends all stared at him with mixed emotions. They all felt awe struck but at the same time they were also angry and offended.

'I have made prayers to the gods on many occasions and I have often had my prayers answered,' said another of his companion as he raised the cup of wine to his lips.

'Enjoy it while it lasts, luck does not last forever.'

Upon hearing the Atheist Soldier's last words his companion dropped his cup suddenly and got to his feet in an instant before reaching out with his hand to grab him.

Another of his friends quickly intervened and kept the two men apart with his hands. 'Enough!' His intervening friend shouted. 'If you really want to spread your blasphemous ways then go to the temple down the street. I heard that the priest there is making a commotion.'

The Atheist Soldier looked around the table and realised his friends were offended by his words and did not want him there. But he was determined to remain defiant. 'Why not. Maybe he can see more sense,' he said. He then picked up his sword from the table and left the inn. He was making his way back to his barracks when he noticed that a small crowd had gathered outside a nearby temple. The priest there was shouting at someone by the temple entrance. When he looked closer, he realised then that the priest was shouting at another one of his fellow soldiers. He recognised him from the armour he wore.

'Go now! Your kind are not welcome here.' Shouted the Priest.

'You're wasting your time with your so-called beliefs. It is better to believe in yourself and accept what is really possible in your own hands than what you fantasise is possible in so called divine intervention.'

'Then how do you explain what is around you? You think people just simply built themselves, or that the sun in the sky was made by beings from this planet? Your ignorance and short sightedness will not go unpunished,' said the Priest.

The people who had gathered around were talking amongst themselves. Words such as "blasphemer", "foolish", "he does not realise that he will die soon" and "his lack of faith will be exposed in the upcoming battle" could be heard amongst the crowd.

'Wait! What he speaks of is not blasphemy or foolishness,' said the Atheist Soldier as he walked forward towards the Priest and his comrade. 'He is simply one who relies on his common sense.'

His comrade looked at him and smiled. 'Thank you.'

'What is the meaning of this?' Asked the Priest.

'It means that he is right in what he says and you are wrong,' said the Atheist Soldier to the Priest.

'And I assume that a non-believer like yourself has a logical explanation as to why you are right and why I am wrong? An explanation based on common sense I hope,' said the Priest, sarcastically.

'Of course I do,' said the Atheist Soldier. 'Would you like me to show you?'

'I can think of no better pleasure,' said the Priest.

'Are you sure you want me to? You may not like it and also I don't want to take responsibility for my actions afterwards.'

The Priest became suspicious. 'Are you planning on killing someone?'

'No, no. Of course not. I promise no one will be hurt. My explanation and proof will be very simple and quick.'

'Then why don't you do it? Show us. Prove to us that our faith in our gods is nothing more than foolhardy fantasy.'

The Atheist Soldier lifted his sword up to his chest and then unsheathed it in an instant. The Priest stared at him nervously but he just looked him straight back in the eyes and grinned. Then he entered the temple and went straight towards the altar. The Atheist Soldier ran straight up the stairs to the altar with his sword in hand and when he reached the top he struck the statue of the god that the temple was dedicated to with one powerful stroke of his blade. The statue fell and smashed onto the floor, bits of it gently flowing over the surface and trickled down the steps to the altar.

The Priest who had just entered the temple a few moments before and witnessed the deed, stared in disbelief and outrage. 'You insolent barbarian! What have you done? You will pay for this!' Shouted the Priest as he ran up the stairs.

'What do you mean pay for it? I only did what you told me to do. You insisted I show you and prove to you why my ideals are correct and I did just that.'

'Desecrating a sacred monument only proves a lack of respect and behaviour equivalent to that of a half-witted savage!'

'Where is your god now? Why isn't he punishing me then for the act of sacrilege I have just committed?'

The Priest stood at the top of the altar looking at the destroyed statue and then looked at the Atheist Soldier. 'You will one day pay for this.'

A group of people had now entered the temple. They all stared in shock and horror at what they saw at the altar.

'Well I am a reasonable man; I will give your god another chance to kill me for this. There will be an important battle in a few days, he will have a chance to kill me then and perhaps even punish us all by having us defeated by the barbarian horde. If it doesn't happen, then I say I have been right all along, that no god exists,' said the Atheist Soldier before he slowly descended the steps.

The people in the temple stared in silence as he made his way out of the temple.

The next day all the soldiers and men who have been conscripted met at their assembly points and then marched on to meet up with the main army in preparation to face the invading force. The battle itself was fierce and bloody. The soldiers all fought bravely and the day was eventually won and the invading force was repelled. After the battle the Atheist Soldier walked around the battlefield with his comrades who were surveying the casualties. During this time, he saw a few metres away from him the soldier who had the argument outside the temple with the priest a few days prior. He raised his sword in acknowledgement of him and he in turn did the same. After the march home the two men saw each other again in the town centre.

'I never got a chance to thank you for the other night. What you did was unnecessary but thank you all the same,' said his comrade as they both walked through town side by side.

'Well if I am honest, I wasn't really trying to help. You see I share the same beliefs as you and I cannot stand it when someone tries to tell me otherwise, it makes you feel oppressed into believing nonsense,' said the Atheist Soldier.

'I understand what you mean. I would love to see the look on that priest's face if he sees us both alive right now,' said his comrade as he looked at him in the eye. They both laughed at the notion. 'Come. Join me for a drink, I will pay the deed. Consider it as payment for your good work the other night.'

Over time the two men became good friends and both believed that the only real goal in life was to live a good life.

A few years later the city was called to arms once again. All soldiers and able-bodied men were again ordered to meet at the relevant assembly points outside the city walls to be ready to march. The Atheist Soldier had just put on his armour and packed all his necessary items, which he took with him. As he was on his way to the assembly point he saw his friend, the one whom he helped outside the temple a few years ago. He was standing outside one of the temples to the gods, he held his sword with the hilt facing vertically upwards in his right hand and his left hand was over his right. He bowed his head slightly with his eyes closed; his posture suggested he was making a rudimentary prayer. As he got closer he heard the words, "God grant me strength", uttered by his friend. His friend then left and made his way to the assembly point with the rest of the soldiers. The two of them stood side by side when the order was given to march.

'I thought you didn't believe in that religious absurdity,' said the Atheist Soldier.

'I don't, but things have changed.' replied his friend.

'Oh, what exactly has changed?'

'I have a wife and child. And this battle we are about to fight is probably the most dangerous so far. I cannot take any more risks, I have to make sure I get all the blessings and luck I can get.'

'The gods don't seem to grant many favours, what makes you think they will grant one for you.'

'I don't. But a possible favour is still better than no favour at all. Don't worry, I do not plan on preaching my new found beliefs onto you my friend. But when you have something as important as I do, you will understand. I am a desperate man now; I am desperate to get back to my family alive.'

The Atheist Soldier did not like what his friend was saying. To him it seemed like his friend was being oppressed by his new found belief but he understood why. If your options for help are limited, then even help from something or someone you don't believe in can hold some value of hope.

When they reached the battlefield the order was given to them to line up in formation, which they did. There they waited for the enemy. Then, when the enemy was spotted, their commander gave the order to raise the shields and lower the spears. A few minutes later the order to advance could be heard and the troops all advanced forward at a walking pace. When the enemy front lines were no more than fifty metres away, they then suddenly charged. The order was given to stand firm with shields and spears at the ready. The enemy charge was fast approaching and within a few seconds the loud and deafening noise of metal clashing with metal could be heard. The soldiers held their ground and thrusted quick and hard with their spears and enemy after enemy soldier fell. The fight seemed too easy and the Atheist Soldier and his comrades began to feel a sense of uncertainty. Then they heard something in the distance, the sound of hooves trampling on ground. As they all feared, it was cavalry charge. The commander shouted out for the rear ranks to change direction and have their spears ready to stop the cavalry from encircling them. The cavalry did not charge directly, they simply came in and made light attacks on the rear ranks, tempting the infantry to break formation.

'Hold formation! Hold Formation!' Some of the soldiers shouted. However, the message did not reach everyone and some of the rear ranks started to break away to engage the attacking cavalry. Now some of the enemy cavalry was in amongst the rear ranks

As the battle raged on, the tide slowly turned in favour of the Atheist Soldier's side. He was exhausted like most of his comrades but he never stopped to think of anything other than his thirst for blood. Then, as a raging enemy soldier came hurling himself towards him with an axe, he thrust his spear forward hard at the chest, the spear point piercing the armour. The enemy soldier stared at him, eyes and lips wide open, teeth clasped together as he let out a loud moan that slowly faded as he fell. Then the Atheist Soldier turned to look behind him and found another enemy soldier charging towards him on horseback, he struggled to free his spear from the dead enemy soldier's armour. As the mounted enemy soldier came closer, screaming with rage until his screams of rage changed to that of pain. He fell from his horse with a spear in his back. When his horse fled, he then saw the figure of his friend, the one who once argued with the priest, standing in the distance before him. As he was about to raise his hand in salute, he saw the expression on his friend's face suddenly change, his mouth opened, his face creased and then he fell. He had been struck from behind. He ran towards his friend's body and stood close by him, fighting with a newfound strength inside.

The battle ended when the day had almost turned to night. The Atheist Soldier looked down at his friend but his body was lifeless despite the eyes being wide open, looking straight at him in a cold unnerving stare. He placed his hand on his dead comrade's forehead. 'I know why now. The gods granted you strength.' He closed his eyes and thought for a moment. For the first time in his life he felt some admiration for someone who had faith in religion. He took one last look at his friend and then slowly brought his hand down over his eyes, closing them as if he could now finally rest in peace. He took his comrade's sword from him and left the battlefield.

When the Atheist Soldier finally arrived back within the city walls, he went straight to his dead friend's house and knocked on the door. When the door opened, he saw a young woman with a child standing beside her, he reached out his hand, holding his friend's sword. 'Is this your husband's sword?' He asked.

'Yes, I recognise it. Where did you get it?'

'I am sorry. But your husband was killed in battle. I saved his sword and brought it to you.'

The woman slowly reached out and took the sword. She held it close to her chest and began to cry.

The Atheist Soldier stayed silent for several moments. 'Your husband fought bravely and he was a good friend too. I can tell you that his virtue is greater than any other man I fought alongside with. Did you know that he was a non-believer in the gods?'

The woman nodded as she wiped away tears. 'Yes. That was one of the things I loved about him. He was always able to see reason beyond religion.'

'Well I can say to you now that you and your child meant so much to him that he was even willing to show faith in the gods in the hope that he would win favour from them to come home to you safely. He asked them to grant him strength, which they did. But he used that strength to save my life on the battlefield. I am sorry,' said the Atheist Soldier before he closed his eyes for a moment and then turned and walked away.

A short while later he came up to a temple he recognised. It was the temple whose altar he desecrated a few years ago. The Atheist Soldier entered the temple and went straight towards the altar. When he reached the steps, he knelt down on his knees and placed his sword next to him on the floor and bowed his head and began to pray. He prayed for a long time.

* * *

When faith can make us realise how important certain things are to us or to those around us, then that faith is worth believing in.

25 - The Time Traveller and His Parents

In the future the known world had united and divided into warring factions, various nations had united with one another against other alliances of other nations. The seven warring factions all fought against one another for control and dominance of the world. The war between the factions went on for many years, until only the Eagle Alliance and The Tears of the Chrysanthemum Factions were left. The two remaining factions fought on for several more years until eventually it would be The Tears of the Chrysanthemum Faction that would prevail. The victory though would come at a great cost in more ways than one, not only was the human cost of the war colossal but much of the territory won from the Eagle Alliance had been made uninhabitable. In the dying days of the war, a bio-chemical weapon had been released upon the lands controlled by the Eagle Alliance. The leaders of The Eagle Alliance feeling the bitterness of defeat and preferring death than living in the shadow of their enemies decided to destroy themselves and their lands. The bio-chemical weapon was released just before the final victory had been achieved.

Over three decades had now passed since the end of the war. All the world's leaders and the remaining members of the former Tears of the Chrysanthemum Faction met in a world summit meeting to discuss current world issues. The discussions were regarding the territories that had been won from the former Eagle Alliance and what must be done about them. Most of the lands were still uninhabitable; many attempts had been made to purify the lands and atmosphere but had so far been unsuccessful. The meeting lasted several days and a solution had been agreed upon by a majority vote on the final day of the meeting. The final hours of the meeting raised a few concerns and some of the leaders wanted their opinions to be heard.

'The solution you're proposing could have severe repercussions,' said one of the leaders.

Another member stood up and responded. 'We are fully aware of that sir, but considering the potential results, we are all agreed that the risk is worth it.'

'Why can't we all agree on a simpler solution? We could just drop powerful armaments from the sky onto the infected areas. It will destroy everything, including the bio-chemical weapon itself,' said another member.

Another member immediately stood up and responded to the last comment. 'The costs associated with such an operation will be too high. We want to be able to reclaim the lands as they use to be and not create another wasteland.'

A long silence filled the hall until eventually the Chairman of the meeting stood. 'Then it is agreed. We will go ahead with Operation History. Dismissed.'

The attendees all got up from their seats and began to leave. The Chairman of the meeting waited by the door and watched each member walk out, he raised his chin slightly when he saw the Minister of National Defence approaching, indicating he wanted to speak with him. 'A quick word minister,' he said.

'Of course,' said the Minister of National Defence.

The two men walked together to the other side of the hall where it was empty and quiet. 'I know I don't have to tell you how important this operation is. But what I really need to know though is how difficult it will be and do you have the resources to make sure it succeeds?' asked the Chairman.

'I understand your concerns sir, the operation will be difficult, I will make no secret of that. Its success will depend almost entirely on the individual we send to carry it out.'

'Do you think you have the right person for this assignment?'

'Yes sir. The man I plan on sending will be perfect'

'How sure are you?'

'I am certain.'

The Chairman stared at him for a moment. 'Good. Proceed with the preparations immediately.'

'Yes sir,' said the Minister of National Defence as he watched the chairman of the meeting leave.

'When will he be ready?' Asked the Minister of National Defence. He stood and watched through the glass windows as the operation was being carried out.

'The operation is almost complete. He will need a few days' rest after that, so he will be ready then.' replied the doctor.

'Good. Notify me when that happens.'

'Understood.'

The operation finished an hour later, the doctors and medics then used a sphygmomanometer to measure the patient's blood pressure to ensure it was stable and then checked the oxygen saturation in his blood. When they were certain his condition was stable they then turned off the lights in the operating room and left the patient to rest.

'Good morning.' A voice called out.

When Ethan awoke he saw a blurred image of an individual standing. Then, when his vision cleared he could see the Minister of National Defence standing before him at the foot of the bed where he lay. Two doctors stood to the left of the Minister of National Defence. He could hear the muffled sounds of their conversation. 'How long have I been out?' asked Ethan as he lay in his bed.

'The operation finished three days ago. You have been resting since. It's good to finally see you awake,' said the Minister of National Defence before he turned his attention to the doctors. 'May we have some privacy please?'

The doctors nodded and then left the room.

'I am pleased to say the operation was a success. I have been informed that your new bionic eyes are working fine as is the time displacement chip in your arm. You now have the ability of night and telescopic vision, as well as the ability to self-replicate artificial retinas. The chip in your arm will link you to the time travelling equipment in the lab allowing you to be placed anywhere in any moment in time in the past or future.'

'Will there be any problems for me in future?'

'There shouldn't be, although we are not entirely sure yet. As you may be aware, not only are you the only agent in the secret service we have tried this on, you are also the very first person to have had this done. Only time will tell.'

Ethan stared at the door directly in front of his bed, as if lost in his thoughts.

The Minister of National Defence waited a moment before speaking to Ethan again. 'There is another matter we must discuss. You remember that we had these operations done on you for a reason?'

Ethan nodded.

'Good. We will discuss what you will be doing soon. Meet me in my office as soon as you feel ready and I will go through the details with you there.' He looked at Ethan again for a moment and then left the room.

The Minster of National Defence sat behind his desk facing Ethan who was sitting directly opposite to him. 'Her name is Doctor Valerie Carter. She was a Biochemist working at the Talon Research Laboratory. I'm afraid we don't have any pictures of her so you will have to identify her yourself when you get there,' he said before pushing a set of documents forward towards Ethan.

Ethan leaned over the table to take the documents from the Defence Minister. As he did this, the small Gold Chrysanthemum shaped pendant he wore around his neck fell out of his shirt.

'That's a beautiful looking pendant you have there. Where did you get it?' asked the Minister of National Defence.

Ethan held the pendant in his hand and looked at it. 'It's a family heirloom. My parents.' He paused for a moment before speaking again. 'My... biological parents left it to me. My adoptive parents said I was found with it.'

'I see.'

There was a moment's silence. 'Is there anything else we know about the target?'

'Yes. We did get some information through interrogating captured enemy officials who worked with her at the time. They say she is about five foot four. Long brunette hair, slim-build. She will in her early thirties in the time period that we are sending you to.'

'So all I have to do is kill her and that will change history?'

'Yes. The records we recovered show that she was definitely the pioneering individual who came up with the bio-chemical weapon that made most of the Eagle Alliance's Territories uninhabitable. If we send you back in time to a period before she began her work on the weapon, you can eliminate her and re-write history. We will still win the war but at the same time, win all the lands of the former Eagle Alliance.'

'Is there anything else I need to know?'

'There is one other thing.' The Minister of National Defence handed Ethan some more documents. 'We have managed to obtain the records of another individual. His name was Edward Thorn; he is not really connected to the target. In fact, other than working at the same lab he is a complete outsider. We know is he due to start working at the Talon Research Laboratory shortly after the time we're planning to send you to. He would be due to attend a job interview there a few days after you arrive, if you can eliminate him first, take his identity and attend his interview for him. That will help you infiltrate the facility and give you free access to locate and identify the main target. Do not worry if you are apprehended by the authorities. The time displacement unit will be automatically set to bring you back exactly four weeks after you arrive, they will not have time for a trial or to have you executed for anything. Just make sure you are alive and we will find you and bring you back. But if you die within the four-week period, the equipment will lose contact with that chip inside you. Just make sure the job is done before anything happens to you.' He looked at Ethan for a while before speaking again. 'So? Any questions?'

'When do we begin?'

'Have you been familiarised with the technology of the time period?'

'Yes.'

'And the geography and environment?'

'Yes.'

'Good. The mission will start tomorrow. We will have everything ready for you. Just be at the lab by 13:00.'

Ethan was briefed on the location and time of where he will be sent and was then taken to the time transportation room. Most of the time displacement technology was in a separate room, the only part that Ethan was allowed to see were the two capsules that would carry him and a suitcase of items he would need on his mission. Instructions were communicated through a loud speaker connected to the time displacement equipment room. It was dark inside the capsule and Ethan tried to relax.

'Close your eyes and try to rest.' A voice called out through the loud speaker.

Ethan lay down and closed his eyes. He tried to rest but the capsule started to become noisy, the sound was similar to an aircraft preparing to take off.

'We are now filling the capsule with the muscle relaxant and time displacement gas.'

Ethan slowly drifted off to sleep, his eyes were closed but he saw a vision of nothing but pure white light, which then faded into darkness. Then the light slowly came back again and then faded back into darkness. This cycle continued over and over again, with the light and darkness disappearing and reappearing quicker with each turn. Then, it was pure white light all around and a voice called out to him.

'You will be safe now. Remember I love you,' said an unfamiliar voice.

Ethan awoke on his back, it was dark and he was in an empty car park in the middle of a downpour. He looked to his left and found the suitcase there, his body was feeling so heavily fatigued that he struggled to get to his feet. He opened the suitcase and quickly pulled out the information regarding Edward Thorn. After looking up his details he hastily pushed the documents back into the suitcase and made his way to the target location.

Ethan located the target's address but did not try to enter immediately. Instead, he sat himself down on a street bench and waited. It was 11:30 pm and he wanted to avoid attracting any unwanted attention. He made himself look like he was waiting for someone to arrive, an act that was not far from the reality of his situation. The streets were empty but many of the houses in the area still had their lights on. He waited patiently until he knew it was the right time to proceed. After waiting for over three hours the last light that he could see within a building finally went out. He picked up the suitcase and began walking towards the house.

Ethan went around to the back of the house and found a patio door, the curtains had not been drawn and he could see there was a study inside. He opened up his suitcase and took out two large oval shaped electro suction pads with handles on them and a laser cutter. He stuck the pads firmly on the glass of the patio door and began cutting the glass whilst holding onto one of the pads.

The house was dark and quiet, Ethan entered the study and quietly looked through every draw in the room and found a passport. He checked the name and date of birth and they matched, he also came across many documents regarding bio-chemical engineering. He was now certain that this was the house of Edward Thorn. Assuming that the man was asleep, he reached into his suitcase and pulled out a facemask, which he put on. He then took out a bottle of hydrogen cyanide and a cloth and then made his way upstairs. He found the man lying on the floor of the bathroom, Ethan looked closely at the face to make sure it was Edward Thorn and it was. The man seemed to be intoxicated and out of consciousness. Ethan stared; he felt a surge of mixed feelings as he opened the bottle and poured a generous amount of liquid into the cloth. He felt relief, pity and guilt as he smothered the cloth onto the man's face until his breathing slowly stopped.

Ethan quickly got out his equipment and began forging and altering the relevant documents. He took hold of the man's face and opened his eyes; he stared into them until his bionic eyes had scanned the man's retinas. He then proceeded to scan Edward Thorn's palms and then uploaded the information into a laptop and then connected the mini three-dimensional printer and started printing out the artificial fingerprints. He later found documents in the study telling him when Edward Thorn was due for a job interview with Talon Research Laboratory. He switched on a nearby computer and checked the time and date, the interview was the next day.

'Well, I believe you could do wonders for us Mr. Thorn and I am glad to tell you that you have got the job,' said the interviewer. 'But you do realise that due to current circumstances with the war against The Tears of the Chrysanthemum Faction, your salary will have to be much lower. I'm afraid funding is limited at the moment.'

'I understand sir.' replied Ethan.

'I can tell you we have checked all your documents and everything seems to be in order. The only thing left to do now is to take a scan of your fingerprints and retinas for the company records. Come with me,' he said and then got up and walked towards the door.

Ethan got up and followed. As they were on their way, a woman was walking towards them in the corridor.

'Doctor Carter!' the interviewer said out loud to the woman. 'I would like you to meet Edward Thorn. He is going to be our new network technician.' the interviewer then turned his attention to Ethan. 'This is Doctor Carter; she is one of our senior Biochemists here. You may as well be acquainted as you will probably run into each other quite a lot.'

'It's good to meet you Mr. Thorn,' said Dr. Carter as she reached out her right hand towards Ethan.

'The feeling is mutual doctor.' replied Ethan as he took her hand. He then looked carefully at her name badge worn over her white coat. The name read clearly as Dr. Valerie Carter. Ethan then quickly examined the rest of her and determined she fit the description given to him at the briefing. He had identified his target. But then, Ethan looked into her eyes and felt something he could not understand. His eyes remained fixated on hers for reasons he could not explain. He did not realise that he was still holding her hand. 'I hope to see you again soon, Doctor Carter.'

Dr. Carter felt uneasy with the staring eyes that Ethan was giving her. She pulled her hand away suddenly and quickly. 'Of course.' she nodded her head slightly and then turned and walked away.

'This way Mr. Thorn, we will quickly take your details down and then everything will be ready.'

Ethan turned his attention back to the interviewer. 'Yes sir, sorry.'

As they both walked down the corridor Ethan turned to look behind him to get one last glance of Dr. Valerie Carter.

Later that day Ethan sat by the window in an old abandoned building near the Talon Research Laboratory. He kept his eyes locked on the entrance to the building and zoomed in with his telescopic vision, making sure he could see every individual who left. He sat waiting patiently for Valerie Carter with a sniper rifle in his hands. He waited for hours until it was almost dark when the figure of a woman slowly came walking out of the building. He zoomed in closer to her face for closer inspection to make sure it was her, as he looked into her face he could see it was without doubt his main target. He aimed the rifle to her head, but then something came over him again and he felt he could not pull the trigger, he hesitated until eventually she was out of sight. Ethan dropped the rifle in a panic trying to find where she had gone, searching frantically with his bionic eyes but there was nothing. He pulled out a handgun from his bag and ran out of the old abandoned building towards the Talon Research Laboratory. His first instincts told him to search the car park, as he looked around he saw a figure standing next to a vehicle and approached it. When he was within a few metres he raised his hand holding the gun and pointed it directly at her. The individual suddenly turned around and looked at him.

Valerie was shocked and leaned her back against the vehicle. The look of fear in her eyes was clear. 'What are you doing? What do you want?' she asked in a quick and fearful tone.

Ethan had the same feeling again as he looked into her eyes. He felt there was something familiar with this woman and the mystery seemed to be in her eyes. Every time he looked into them he got this feeling. A feeling which told him that he had seen those eyes before, but where? He stood there in silence, still aiming the gun towards Dr. Carter but not being able to pull the trigger. His mind wondered off in search, just where had he seen those eyes before? Then a picture of himself standing in front of a mirror came into his mind. 'Yes.' He thought to himself. 'That is where I have seen those eyes before, I have seen them in me, my own reflection. Before the operation for these bionic eyes.' Then suddenly his vision quickly faded and all was suddenly dark.

Valerie took a deep breath and then ran towards the individual holding the gun and hugged him. 'Thank you sir, thank you, thank you so much,' she said in a quick and relieved tone as she held the man who just saved her life.

'Do you know who he was Doctor?' asked the armed security guard. He had seen what had happened in the car park from within the building and quickly came to intervene. He was armed and shot Ethan in the head.

'Not really. All I know is that his name is Edward Thorn, I was introduced to him earlier and he looked at me strangely,' said Dr. Carter.

'An obsessed individual I assume. Are you all right?'

Valerie nodded.

'Come, its best we get you inside now.'

The two left the car park and went back inside the laboratory building, leaving Ethan's dead body lying where it was.

Over a year had passed and the war against The Tears of the Chrysanthemum Faction was nearing its end. The city was under an air strike and there were few safe places for anyone to hide. Doctor Valerie Carter was at home with her husband and her three-week-old baby son.

'It has to be done Valerie and now we don't have much time,' said Valerie's husband.

'Please. Just let me spend one last hour with him.' pleaded Valerie as she held her son in her arms.

'You can't! I must take him to safety. He will be safe I promise.'

'Where will you take him?'

'Enemy territory, I know people who can smuggle him there safely.'

'But what if they kill him on sight?'

'We will leave him this,' said her husband as he pulled out a gold pendant shaped like a chrysanthemum. 'Hopefully this will be enough to fool anyone who finds him that he is of noble birth. From an important family of The Tears of the Chrysanthemum Faction.'

Valerie began to cry uncontrollably and held the child close. 'I can't!'

'If you love him as much as you say you do then you know you have to do this.'

Valerie cried again for a few moments and then nodded.

Her husband placed the pendant on the child's chest and held her.

Valerie took one last look at her child before speaking. 'You will be safe now. Remember I love you.' As she looked at her child, a single tear fell from her left eye and landed on the gold pendant.

Her husband then took the child from her and left the house.

* * *

Feelings of connection, important emotions and bonds that are true can never be changed. No matter how time is altered and displaced.

26 - The Time Traveller and The Great Auk

A great scientist invented a portable time machine and a teleportation device that could transport him anywhere in the world. He had dedicated many years of his career to invent and build these devices because he was fascinated by history and wanted to see all the greatest events, monuments that mankind had built, lost treasures and extinct creatures of the past.

He connected the two devices together to have them both work simultaneously and then he set the time and area for his first time travelling journey. St Kilda, Scotland. 1710 AD. The time traveller was nervous, this was the first time he had tested the device and he was not certain on what the outcome would be. He rested his thumb on the activation button for a few seconds and then pressed it. Then the world seemed to have gone silent and darkness filled every space, the Time Traveller felt like he was standing on air and the empty space around him felt like it was moving. Then, it felt like it was moving faster and faster, then everything stopped and the world slowly came to light again.

He found himself standing near the shores of St Kilda in Scotland. It was a clear and peaceful day and the sound of the waves could be heard. The Time Traveller began walking and looked around, he took great pleasure in enjoying the scenic view of rocks and vegetation but then something extraordinary happened. A black and white bird came out from behind a rock, the Time Traveller had never seen anything like it before but he knew straight away what it was. The bird just walked around casually, seemingly without a care in the world despite the Time Traveller being close by. It was obvious that it had no natural fear of humans. It was approximately thirty inches tall, the feathers on its belly were white, whilst the feathers on its small wings and back were black with black webbed feet. It had a large black beak and its wings appeared small in proportion to its plump body size.

'The Great Auk,' said the Time Traveller as he stared at it. He had learnt about this animal in his own time but it had been extinct since the nineteenth century, neither he nor anyone of his time had ever seen one. He kept looking at it in admiration, he knew there was much more that history had to offer but his fascination with this creature kept him from travelling to another time.

The Time Traveller lit a fire by nightfall and kept himself warm. After sitting by the fire for a few minutes, he found himself being surrounded by several great auks; the fire seemed to attract them to come near. Some of them took a slight interest in him and got closer to examine, others just walked around or sat near the fire and made themselves comfortable. The Time Traveller enjoyed their company; he sat resting his left arm on his left knee which was bent with the sole of his left foot on the ground. He watched the great auks sitting by the fire, some of them sleeping and the light from the fire illuminating parts of their bodies. He looked on, comforted by the warmth of the fire and the relaxing sight until eventually his head slowly lowered until his chin almost touched his throat and he drifted off to sleep.

When the Time Traveller awoke he found that the fire had died out and the great auks were all gone. He stood up to begin his next time travelling journey and set the time and place for 3000 BC, Wiltshire, England. He wanted to see the construction of Stonehenge, he imagined in his own mind how it would look and then pressed the activation button. When he arrived there he was amazed again. Fascinated by the techniques and strength of the workers hauling the huge stones to construct this famous monument. He was even more amazed when he eventually saw it completed in all its glory and finally learning what the monument was used for.

Over the course of several weeks, the Time Traveller had seen and witnessed many spectacular things. The Battle of Marathon at Greece and the magnificent achievement of Pheidippides. The construction of the Great Pyramid and the wonder of how it looked. The Hanging Gardens of Babylon. The harsh and amazing last ice age. The Neanderthals and their co-existence with Homo Sapiens. And many more.

After the many journeys he decided it was time for him to return home. But just as he thought of that, he could not remember where home was. He looked through the recorded times that he had travelled to on his time travelling device but it did not tell him much, for it only records the time periods that he had travelled to and not from. The first entry was, St Kilda, Scotland, 1710 AD. His instincts told him to go to a time after then so he set the time and place for St Kilda, Scotland, 1750 AD. When he arrived there, he found himself standing near the shores of St Kilda in Scotland. It was a clear and peaceful day and the sound of the waves could be heard. Then he saw something come out from behind some rocks, it was The Great Auk again. He remembered this bird and being fascinated by it. He walked up close and examined it, he remembered the night he spent here and the fire and the many great auks surrounding him but nothing else. The time traveller remained there for the rest of his life. He never made it home.

* * *

People who only think of the past and become fixated with it will forget all that there is in the present and will spend their future in the past.

27 - The Spirits and The Duellist

A man by the name of Evangelos had accepted a duel in principle because his challenger was the man who was responsible for the death of his father and many of his friends. But a few days before the duel was due to start he began to have doubts in his ability to win. He felt that defeat would be inevitable and he would dishonour himself and all those who have gone before him. He was also fearful for his life and kept picturing himself dead on the ground after losing the duel to his opponent.

The next day he was practicing his swordsmanship with a colleague, they practiced in a large hall with mirrors on one side and windows on the opposite side. He practiced hard but he could not concentrate. Each time they began he would drop his sword after a few strokes or he would be caught off guard. They began again but the moment they started his colleague had disarmed him easily.

'What is happening?' asked his colleague. 'You were better a few weeks ago.'

'I am afraid.' he replied.

'Why? You are a good swordsman, better than your father ever was and anyone else I know.'

He fell to his knees to pick up his sword. 'There is too much at stake here. My family's honour is at stake and those close to me who have died, I fear disappointing them even though they are not here.'

'Then concentrate, you cannot honour the dead by giving up on life.'

Feeling the importance of his purpose he felt his courage renewed. He picked up his sword and took up his position again. 'You are right, let's begin again.' He lunged forward with a thrust but his colleague saw it coming and parried the thrust to the right quickly and pressed forward with just his arm as Evangelos was still lunging towards him. Direct hit to the torso. He looked down slightly and saw the blunt point of his colleague's sword resting on his chest. He dropped his sword in disappointment. 'I am lucky these are only practice swords.' Then he saw from the edge of his eye something moving in the mirror. He turned his head to look in the mirror but could only see himself and his colleague.

'Lucky strike,' said his colleague. 'Again?'

He looked at his colleague but then felt there was someone standing by the window. He turned his attention to the window but saw nothing. He began taking off his armour. 'No, not today. Maybe tomorrow.'

'The duel is in two days. Are you sure you have time to waste?'

He did not respond and walked away.

'Evangelos!' Shouted his colleague.

But Evangelos did not respond.

That night Evangelos heard several voices calling out to him.

'What are you afraid of?' A strange echoing but familiar voice called out to him

'What are you afraid of?' Another strange voice called out.

These same words kept repeating themselves over and over again. Each time with a different voice that echoed in his ear.

Evangelos woke from his sleep. His entire body sweating, his breathing was heavy and barely controllable. He looked around the room inspecting it to make sure there was nothing unusual in the house and when he was certain there wasn't, he lay back down but was unable to sleep.

The next morning Evangelos was on his way to the practice hall, he noticed the door to the practice hall had been left open and he could see from the mirrors that it was empty. He stopped just outside to put on his protective suit. As he was changing he thought he caught a glimpse of something in the practice room moving, when he turned his attention to the mirrors he saw that a practice sword had been left, rolling around on the floor. He went in to have a look and found one of the windows open and a breeze was coming in.

'You're early.' A voice called out from behind.

Evangelos turned around and saw his colleague whom he was practicing with yesterday. He was already suited up and looked ready to begin fencing. 'You were right yesterday. I do not have much time, so I wanted to get an early start.'

'Shall we begin?' asked his colleague.

Evangelos nodded.

They practiced for many hours, although his swordplay had improved since the previous day, it was still not good enough to make him believe he could win. His colleague continuously out-fenced him with each duel, it seemed the harder he tried the quicker he would lose. He tried to slow the tempo but it only seemed to delay the inevitable, the outcome was still the same. They stopped practicing when Evangelos looked out the window and realised that it was nearly dark.

'You should go home,' said his colleague. 'get plenty of rest before the meeting tomorrow.'

Evangelos just nodded in acknowledgement but could not even look at his colleague and just made his way to the exit door. Whilst on his way home he thought about the duel the next day, he kept picturing in his mind how the duel would play out. And each time he pictured the duel, the outcome was a picture of him, defeated and dead. He kept picturing it again and again and the outcome was still the same. After thinking about the same thing for over an hour he then stopped walking and looked around, he found himself alone on a long straight path with trees on either side. He was not where he was supposed to be and found himself lost. He began to walk again but at a slower pace. He kept looking at either side of the path, looking beyond the trees for something he would recognise to set him on the right path again, but there was nothing. Evangelos kept walking slowly.

'Evangelos.' An unknown echoing voice called out.

The sound startled Evangelos and he suddenly turned around quickly to see what was behind him. But there was nothing there. He looked in every direction but could see nothing.

'Evangelos.' Another strange voice called out.

Again Evangelos looked behind to see who or what it was that said that but still there was nothing. When he turned back to face what was in front of him, he saw several ghostly figures standing before him, the figures were translucent and they all stared at him. Out of impulse he reached out to touch one of them but his hand just went straight through the individual figure. Evangelos's hands began to shake and twitch and he slowly began to step backwards, then out of panic he turned and ran. He ran for what seemed like an eternity without ever looking back, when he thought he had covered enough ground he stopped and looked behind him but there was nothing, then when he turned back, they were there again. 'WHO ARE YOU? WHAT DO YOU WANT?' He shouted but there was no answer. Out of instinct he turned to his right and ran straight into the trees, he ran as fast as he could and now found himself surrounded in a forest of trees. He changed direction and ran again but it seemed like he was going nowhere, then he tried to turn back to the direction he came but no matter how far and fast he ran there just seemed to be no end to this forest. He fell to the ground on his hands and knees exhausted, breathing heavily and struggling for breath.

'Why are you afraid?' Another voice cried out.

Evangelos looked up and saw the ghostly figure of his dead father. He pushed himself back, landing his buttocks; he could now see the familiar faces of his dead father and many of his old friends. He frantically tried to distance himself away from them pushing himself back with his hands and feet until he felt the hard surface of a large tree trunk pressing against his back.

'Why are you afraid of us?' asked his father.

'You're... you're dead father, you are all dead. Why are you here?'

'You fear us because we should be dead?'

'Yes, you are not of this world, why do you...'

'No Evangelos. You are afraid because you believe we are here.'

'What?'

'Your fear is in your beliefs. Rid yourself of those beliefs and your fear will disappear.'

'I don't understand?'

'Where did you believe you were going before you saw us?'

'Home.'

'And where is home?'

Evangelos thought for a moment and then closed his eyes, he kept his eyes closed for several seconds, trying to clear his mind and when he opened them, he found himself outside his house. He looked at his house, then he thought about what the ghostly figure of his father had told him. He finally understood now and knew what must be done.

The next day he met his opponent at the agreed secluded area just outside the city. Before the duel was to begin, he thought about the previous night's events. He just stood where he was, sword in hand in sixte position and did not move, even when the signal was given to begin. His opponent was confused and intimidated, wondering what his intentions were. Evangelos realised now that he feared defeat and death simply because that was what he believed in. Then suddenly he thought of striking his opponent, he lunged forward quickly and suddenly after standing completely still for several moments. His opponent had no time to respond and the tip of Evangelos's blade came to rest on his opponent's throat. His opponent dropped his sword and raised his hands in defeat.

* * *

The chances for success can be greatly increased when one can believe in one self to succeed instead of believing that one would fail.

28 - The Artist and His Work

There was once a great artist who was relatively unknown to the world during his lifetime. He had dedicated almost his entire life to practicing and perfecting the visual arts and during those years he had painted and drawn thousands of paintings and pictures, all of which done with divine precision. He also sculpted several statues and objects based on all kinds of artistic thinking, for he did not just create works of art based on what his eyes could tell him but also on what he could sense and feel. He once painted the surging waves throughout the body, his expression of what love would look like if it could be seen. He also sculpted the statue of feeling, his expression of how joy would look like, if it were tangible.

Over the years the artist rarely managed to sell any of his work but he kept working and striving to keep bettering himself in what he did. But then, towards the end of his life he began losing his ability to do what he loved most, old age and illness had taken its toll on the man and his work began to deteriorate. He used what money he had left and borrowed more from friends and family who cared for him to have his work preserved. He rented a storehouse and placed all his work there for safekeeping. The man loved his work and took great pride in what he had in his ability as an artist. Being surrounded by works of art that he himself had created only reminded him of who he once was and how great he used to be and ultimately, what he had lost. The pain of that was too much and he soon forgot his glorious past and died peacefully in his sleep.

After the artist passed away his work remained in the storehouse for several months, gathering dust and seemingly forgotten by the world. Then one day his work was moved to another location. Much of it though was lost due to careless handling and also by thoughtless people who cared little for art and simply just threw much of his work away. However, some of the work was saved and placed in a warehouse where it remained for several years.

Then one day his work was being moved again, this time one of the people responsible for this task was a great practitioner and admirer of art himself. He viewed the work he saw with great admiration and was inspired by them and felt that the world needed to see the work that he himself was looking at. He decided to contact curators, museums and even colleges and universities regarding the work that he had just discovered in the hope that they would be interested in acquiring and preserving them. After some inspection, some of them were in fact interested and decided to take the work for exhibits and for general safe keeping.

In the years that followed saw the great artist's work being greatly admired around the world and finally he had been given the recognition that he so greatly deserved but had so long been denied. Not only was his work admired but it was also used to teach future generations of artists on what true art stood for and meant. The great artist's work helped encourage many young and upcoming artists to work hard and strive to become all that they can be. Some even went on to become the epitome of the great artist himself.

Good things that are saved from the past can help to serve good in the present and the future.

29 - The Meerkat and The Ground Squirrel

There was once a meerkat called Light Fur who felt that he was of no value to his clan. He felt that his analysis was justified because of the entire clan of twenty-four members he was the one who dug the slowest. Whenever new tunnels and entrances in their burrow were required to be dug, he always found that his colleagues could dig much faster than him. While they could dig their own body weight in dirt in just a few seconds, it takes him at least twenty seconds to achieve the same feat. Whenever they were out foraging, it was always him that found the least amount of food, so much so that sometimes he had to rely on his contemporaries just to have enough to eat for himself. His shortcomings made him feel depressed and without a sense of belonging as he viewed himself as a burden to the clan.

One day he was placed on sentry duty whilst the rest of the clan were out of the burrow looking for food. He stood upright on his hind legs and tail and looked out into the distance, staying vigilant on his lookout for potential danger. Because he felt that he had so far fallen short of expectations for his clan, he watched hard and carefully, determined to do good this time. He watched over the distance and moved his eyes to scan every area and direction of the ground. He watched every bush, tree, rock and moving object with strong-minded detail, he even looked out for disturbances or irregularities in the sand. His hard work and diligence seemed to have been more than sufficient at first but he made one critical error. Because he had concentrated his efforts so much on the ground, he had forgotten to look out for any threats coming from the sky. Then suddenly, he heard the frantic screaming from some members of his clan running back towards the burrow and alerted all the other meerkats that there was danger. A bird of prey had swooped down from the sky and tried to snatch a member of his clan, luckily the quick reaction and quick thinking of his companion saw him run straight into the gap between two rocks shielding him from the predator. The rest of the clan all made it back into the burrow before the bird of prey had a chance to try and snatch one of them.

Inside the burrow the lead male of the clan was furious at what just happened.

'What happened? Who was on sentry duty?' shouted the Lead Male.

Light Fur slowly came forward. 'I was sir.'

'You! You useless incompetent! Isn't there anything you can get right? You're a useless digger, a useless forager for food and now you're also a useless sentry. We would be better off if you were dead!'

The rest of the clan stared in silence. Their eyes moving from the lead male to Light Fur every few seconds.

One of his other companions stepped forward and spoke for him. 'That wouldn't be a good idea. There are other clans who are bigger and stronger than us who live nearby. We cannot afford to lose anyone, no matter how useless he or she is. The extra numbers alone can act as a sign to show strength in numbers.'

'Very well, you can stay. For now. Now go and check to see if the danger is over and make sure you get it right this time,' said the Lead Male.

Light Fur immediately went to the entrance and peered through, he felt disheartened from the words of the clan leader that he took no precautions for his own safety. He stepped out of the burrow and looked around, this time he made sure he checked the skies as well and all seemed clear. Then, as Light Fur was still making his observation, the member of his clan who hid himself in the rocks came running towards him. 'Are you all right?'

'Yes. The bird that attacked us is gone. I saw it fly off with a lizard clasped in its talons. It should not be back in hurry,' said his companion.

'Everything is clear!' he shouted into the burrow.

The rest of the clan began leaving the burrow and Light Fur stood guard by the entrance again.

'No. Not you. I need someone who can do the job properly,' said the Lead Male after coming out of the burrow. 'You!' He shouted at another member of the clan as he was walking away from the burrow.

The other clan member came running towards the Lead Male and stopped in front of him.

'Take his place,' he said to the other clan member, gesturing that he wanted him to be on sentry duty instead. He then turned his attention to Light Fur. 'You go look for food.'

Without delay Light Fur went on his way, trying to keep his eyes away from the Lead Male, still feeling ashamed of his earlier mistake. He deliberately strayed far from the burrow and every member of his clan, feeling the need to be alone and away from others to reflect on himself. He found himself a quiet spot on a rock by a small pool of water. He sat himself on the rock and then looked into the water, staring at his reflection. A few minutes later he heard an unfamiliar sound rustling in the bush just opposite the pool, he immediately looked up and stared at the bush, sensing that danger was nearby. He placed his forelimbs and hind limbs on the ground, readying himself to make a quick getaway. Then a small figure came out of the bush and his fear soon vanished. It was an old Ground Squirrel carrying a lot of vegetation and fruit in his hands. He casually approached Light Fur and sat next to him on the rock.

'Good morning my friend. You do not mind me sitting here do you?' asked the Ground Squirrel as he put the items he was carrying down and began feeding.

'Well if you consider me your friend then I am more than happy to have you sit with me. You're the only friend I have at the moment.'

'Really. Why? I thought you meerkats lived in large groups.'

'Yes we do. But my group are not too warm towards me right now because I am worthless to them. And to be fair I agree with them.'

The Ground Squirrel started going through the food he had foraged and picked out some seeds and began gnawing at them. 'Why they not like you?' he asked, in between bites.

'I offer little benefit to my clan. I am no good at finding food, I can't dig very well and I can't even carry out the task of sentry duty without causing trouble.'

The Ground Squirrel went through his stash of food again and picked out some berries. 'Here,' he said as he handed the berries to Light Fur. 'I know you meerkats prefer insects in your diet but I'm afraid I don't have any. But I heard you're also quite fond of fruits.'

Light Fur took the berries gratefully. 'Thank you,' he said and then began eating hastily. He was very hungry by now.

'It takes time to find yourself in this world my friend. We are all unique, even amongst our own peers. None of us can do the same thing to exactly the same level as the next individual.'

Light Fur was chewing a berry and then swallowed slowly. 'Well for some of us we have to find our form soon. It's a very fast and competitive world we live in unfortunately and if I don't find something useful to do soon, I could end up alone or isolated.' Light Fur looked down at his reflection again whilst holding a half-eaten berry.

'Well having so much doubt about yourself and rushing things through will not help you get there any faster,' said the Ground Squirrel and then took another few bites of the seeds and chewed for a few seconds before speaking again. 'Like me, in my group I am the one who is most capable of finding food, it's my specialty. But I have not always been good at it, it took a long time for me to develop my abilities in foraging. I learnt over time that the best place to find vegetation is in places where the soil is richest and where water is in plentiful supply. It also helps to listen to other animals and see if you can find out where there has been rain recently. Where there is water and fertile ground, there will be food.'

Light Fur listened intently. 'How do you know all this?'

'I know because I pay attention to what happens all around me and I listen to others. What you can contribute to the world requires work, time and patience. Just remember it rarely happens instantly, you need to give it time to find and explore all your capabilities. It's almost a game of chance, just wait and be patient and a chance will come,' said the Ground Squirrel and he began chewing on some roots that he found earlier.

Light Fur thought for a moment and felt rejuvenated by the wise squirrel's words. 'Thank you sir, for your kind and inspirational words. They have helped me a lot already.'

'Oh it's all right. We Ground Squirrels could do with more friendly animals like you meerkats around; we have no issues with one another and can co-exist peacefully. You also make very good lookout posts, you meerkats seem to know how to spot dangers.'

Light Fur thanked the Ground Squirrel again for his kind words and then made his way back to his burrow. As he neared the burrow he heard loud sounds of distress, screams and shrieks of pain and physical struggling came echoing out of the burrow. Light Fur immediately broke into a frantic run. When he reached the entrance to the burrow he noticed that the sentry was no longer standing guard and there was no one else around thus he stormed his way in. Letting his ears guide him in his search, he followed the sound of the screams, turning left and then turning right, running through tunnel after tunnel, searching chamber after chamber. Then finally, he came to the sleeping chamber where he found the sentry guard and the Lead Male trying to defend the burrow and two meerkat pups against four other meerkats from another clan. The fighting was fierce, the sentry was down and the Lead Male was seriously injured, his left eye and left hind leg were both bleeding. One of the intruding meerkats leapt on him and pinned him down while another was about to deliver the death blow. Light Fur acted quickly and hurled himself onto the back of one of the intruders, sinking his teeth and claws into his neck, the intruder fell and died on the spot. Then before the other three intruding meerkats could react, Light Fur jumped towards one of them whilst the other two fighting the Lead Male looked on, digging his claws into the intruder's neck and thigh and wrestling him to the ground. The clan sentry who was still down then sensed an opportunity and struck one of the other intruding meerkats from behind, pinning him to the ground and biting into his back. The last intruder still holding down the clan's Lead Male began to panic as he realised that the odds were no longer in his favour. He quickly let go of the clan's Lead Male in fear and ran out of the burrow as quickly as he could. When his two companions realised he had gone they too made a quick escape.

As the dust settled inside the burrow, Light Fur and the sentry guard inspected the rest of the burrow, making sure that no more rival clan members were still lying in wait within the tunnels and chambers. When they were certain that there were no more of them they then attended to each other. The pups and Light Fur himself had luckily come out of it unscathed, the sentry guard suffered just light cuts and scratches but the Lead Male was seriously wounded.

'It was fortunate that you arrived when you did. If you had come any later then I don't think he would have lived,' said the sentry to Light Fur whilst gesturing towards the Lead Male.

'What happened?' asked Light Fur.

'It appears that our unwanted guests had been watching the burrow for a while. When they saw you leave and there was only the two of us standing by the entrance, they suddenly came running towards the burrow. We tried to fight them off before they got to the entrance but there were too many and one of them managed to get past and entered the burrow, so the Lead Male went in after him and I followed.'

'Maybe next time we should have more sentries posted. Stay here with him, I will inform the others,' said Light Fur.

A few days later, after the incident with the intruding rival clan members, the clan were coming out of the burrow to forage for food again. Light Fur was on sentry duty; he stood to attention and watched each member of the clan coming out. After a short while he noticed that everyone had left the burrow with the exception of the Lead Male. He felt curious as he knew that he had by now recovered from his injuries. Then when everyone else was out of sight he saw the shape of the Lead Male emerging from the burrow, as he came out he stopped next to Light Fur.

'Thank you for saving me and my children the other day. And I wish to apologise for some of the words I used against you earlier that day,' said the Lead Male.

'There is no need for the apology. What you said that day was not an incorrect assessment of my contribution to the clan and I always appreciate being told the truth.'

'Maybe so, but you proved me wrong in the end. Therefore, my comments about you that day were eventually wrong.'

Light Fur could not think of a response.

'I want you to know that despite your shortcomings, I have great faith in you protecting the clan against outside threats. What you did the other day proves you put the wellbeing of the clan before your own life and I cannot ask for any more than that. If we are ever threatened again I have belief in you that you would succeed in protecting the clan.'

Light Fur looked at the Lead Male and closed his eyes for a moment as a mark of acknowledgement and appreciation. The Lead Male then left to forage. Light Fur stood to attention and looked out into the distance.

* * *

This fable shows two things:

One should not always judge one's worth by making comparisons of how much or how well one can do in a particular discipline in comparison to others. As individuals we are all unique in what we do and we can therefore be different in what we can contribute to the world.

Whenever one should feel that they are worthless then one should ask someone who knows them well if they have faith in them to do something important if the situation required it. If others should hold faith in another individual, then that faith could one day be worth more than anything else they have or can turn to. There can be no greater gift if an individual needs another.

30 - Life, Death and Hope

When a child has just been born into the world, its cries and movements are viewed with fascination. Just how is life so suddenly made and given? To most, life is a miracle. Meanwhile in another part of the world, a man was dying. He lay on his deathbed waiting for death to come and claim him; it was a moment of sorrow. He was a good man, adored by his friends and family, they all looked on and wondered why such a man must face death. They did not want him to go, they loved him. His final wish was to die in the company of those he cared about and for them to be with him even after death itself.

Life and Death oppose one another. Neither understands the work of the other and they only appreciate their own work.

'You instil death into all living creatures and I instil life into them,' said Life.

'Is it not that this world requires us both to do our deeds?' asked Death.

'Of course, but what I give is a gift to the world, you simply take that gift from them in your deeds.'

'I do what I must. Isn't it when one life is taken another is given?'

Life did not answer that last question. 'You fill every living creature with emotions like anger, aggression, irrational behaviour and jealousy to encourage them to kill or die themselves.'

'Just as you do yourself. The emotions I instil the world may cause death but you also use them to advance life. Such emotions can be used in many ways, I just happen to use them to create death, you use them to create life.'

The two gazed upon one another for a moment and then parted ways.

Over time Life and Death continued throughout the world. Everywhere Life fed emotions into living creatures such as pride, to encourage individuals to procreate as fertility and offspring were a sign of creation and good work. Lust, causing uncontrollable desires to copulate. And of course love, the desire for affection and compassion, leading to individuals wanting something to represent each other. But Life also instils the less conventional emotions, irrational behaviour, causing some to copulate for no real reason or to copulate for revenge and retaliation. Jealousy, bringing life into the world that others would not approve of.

But where there is Life is also Death. And Death also instils emotions into living creatures to bring about death. Jealousy, aggression and even love to encourage individuals to take life from others. Irrational behaviour to shorten one's life span. And emotions that encourage aging.

As Life and Death spread throughout the world, creatures of all kinds lived and died each day but as this cycle ran its course, it seemed that Life was succeeding more than death could. There were more creatures born each day than there were ones who died. Life expectancy was also increasing and everyone just seemed to live longer and longer. Death grew envious of the success of Life, it seemed that his work was better or more efficient than his and he wanted that to change. One day Death sought out Life and found him standing in the middle of a forest looking into the sky. Death wondered what Life was doing and he soon found his answer, for the sky began to rain. Life had just instilled the emotions of love and maternal instinct into the sky, bringing forth the life giving nourishment of her tears down onto the world, giving life to the forests and all living creatures.

'There is too much life in this world. You should not work so hard to put too much of it here,' said Death.

'Maybe there is too much life because there is just not enough death. You should work harder to keep the balance.' replied Life.

'Your work is long and difficult. Maybe you should rest.'

'I rest as and when I wish. Right now I have work to do.'

'I think there is too much life in the world now.'

'Then what do you suggest?' asked Life.

Death looked up into the sky. The thoughts of anger and aggression filled him, then he focused those emotions into the sky. Lightning then struck down onto the forest, several bolts at a time, setting fire to the forest and then thunder roared across the lands as if the sky was screaming in pain and anger. 'I will start by destroying this forest.'

Life looked Death in the face. 'What are you implying here?'

'My intention now is to destroy all life.'

'And how do you propose to do that?'

Death stared back at Life and for a few moments there was silence. 'Just wait and it will happen.' His solemnity was obvious and then Death disappeared.

Life calmed himself and urged a sense of peace throughout his thoughts and then instilled these emotions into the sky. The storm stopped and all was now peaceful. He stood in the forest in silence, thinking and trying to comprehend exactly what Death's plans were in destroying life. He thought for a long time, not realising that the time that had passed for him was much more significant in the world where he creates life, until eventually, he gave up in his search for the answer.

When he returned to the world of mortal beings he found Death had taken a heavy toll on the world. Many had died during his time spent absent from his work, nothing grew and nothing had been born but many were dead or dying. Life immediately tried to put life back into the world, but something was wrong. It seemed that few beings wanted to live or procreate. He watched one pair of mortal beings coming together and then instilled emotions of love and desire into them to entice them into a passionate embrace but nothing happened. He tried again with others but only being able to succeed after trying many times. Life then tried to fill every living animal's mind with pride, wanting them to produce offspring as a sign of dominance and prosperity but that only produced limited results. Even the sky refused to rain and the sun refused to produce the life giving warmth it has always done. All living beings were fighting amongst themselves and behaving irrationally. Famine and disease soon spread throughout the world. Life could not understand what was causing it all.

Then he noticed something. A man lay dying on the ground with others surrounding him.

'Don't let me die in vain,' he said. 'Fight on and do not give up, that is our only hope.' His eyes then slowly closed and death claimed him as well. The ones around him then rose up and ran towards another group of men and fought each other until no more blood could be spilled.

Then Life witnessed another dying man's words.

'After I am gone, I hope you too will die a noble death,' he said to his companion who held him in his arms. Then as he breathed his last breath, a group of men approached the dead man and his companion and attacked the dead corpse. The dead man's companion fought back and tried to protect his body from harm, until he too was killed.

Life stopped and thought about the two dying men's last words and one word kept echoing back to him. Hope.

'Both of them mentioned this word, but why?' He thought to himself. He thought for a bit longer and then he realised what had happened. There is no hope for life, only death. Hope had been turned away from Life and now she favours Death.

He now sought out Death. He needed to find him before all hope for life was lost. He searched the world over but could not find his adversary anywhere. He searched on and all the while, Life continued to perish until he fell with exhaustion.

'I know you have been looking for me,' said Death.

Life stirred in his sleep and then awoke. He looked at Death and then noticed there was someone else standing with him. It was a feminine figure, very beautiful, dark haired and slender. 'It's you. The Hope that has been missing in life.' Life rose to his feet and stared at Hope. 'Why are you helping him? Why do you destroy what lives only for you?'

Hope stared at him in the face, emotionless and did not answer.

'You have been seduced by him. But you can still turn back, don't let this world die. It is as beautiful as you are, such beauty is not easily made and you can't just let it all disappear.'

'Beauty is in the eye of the beholder. This is not the only time that the world had faced so much death, it is only natural for it to happen again,' said Death.

'You only do this out of envy for my good work. You think that if there is more death than there is life then that makes you superior but it only makes you a source of evil,' said Life.

'You don't understand do you? You say this is a beautiful world but do you even realise how the world became so beautiful?'

Life stayed silent and did not answer.

Hope continued to stare at Life and then lowered her eyes and looked to the ground, almost as if in regret.

'The world is beautiful because it evolves and changes. Change can only happen when what was before is no more. Only then would there be room for change and change leads to beauty,' said Death.

'I have worked too hard to make this world what it is and I will not let you destroy it,' replied Life. He rushed in to try and take Hope away from Death but just as he was within reach, Hope looked up and stared at him in the face, her eyes suddenly glowing and Life fell to the ground again, this time in great pain. Life screamed and shouted, twisting and shaking on the ground. Every part of him was in a sudden shock and the pain surged through him, almost like lightning striking him from the inside. Then his vision failed him and there was darkness.

When he awoke, the world had turned into a barren wasteland. Almost nothing lived, what was left of life was now scattered in small parts around the world. He looked on in despair but he refused to give up. He slowly started his work again and began supporting life, instilling the emotions required to start life again. His work seemed in vain, whatever he did seemed to make little difference and all Hope for Life seemed lost.

Life fell to his knees and closed his eyes. He imagined what the world use to be and held onto that image, not wanting to open his eyes and face reality. Then, suddenly he felt something taking hold of him from behind. The warm feeling of hands slowly spread from his waist up to his chest, he opened his eyes and looked behind him. Hope had finally returned and she was now by his side.

'I am sorry for what has happened to this world. But I can only support you and others so much before I have to leave and support another cause,' said Hope.

'There is little or nothing now. It is too late to bring back what has now gone,' said Life.

Hope held onto him tight and together they rose to their feet. 'It is never too late. There is still life left and I am here now.'

Life turned around to face Hope.

'Now the world we used to have is gone, we can now start over and build a new one,' said Hope and then closed her eyes.

From that moment on, Hope finally embraced Life with all her passion and together they stood.

Over several years, with Hope on his side, Life slowly began to recover. The sun began to shine brighter, the sky started to give life-nourishing rain again and forests began to regrow. Animals slowly repopulated the world and the oceans were once again filled with life.

* * *

When life and death come into conflict with one another one must understand that both are connected in a way that both require hope to sustain them. We all live with the hope of positive outcomes in life and when we die there is always hope in our minds of the positive aspects of death, such as the hope that we can die in peace or that death can bring us peace. Hope should never be reserved only for life or only for death, for as long as we have to live and die then hope is required even in death as it is in life.

31 - The Dinosaurs and Humankind

Dinosaurs rule the world because they are the most advanced beings on Earth. They dominate because of their extreme size and strength, they overpowered every other land creature in every way. They are more intelligent and they also have speed, allowing them to outcompete any other animal in the world.

In what is now North America, in the region of Alberta Canada, a dromiceiomimus was feeding on an egg she had just snatched from a lambeiomimus nest. Such a raid on a lambeosaurus nest was a bold one, for these creatures are forty feet long and weigh over five tons. An enraged lambeosaurus mother would show no mercy to a twelve-foot long and two hundred pound dromiceiomimus. But due to her very quick and agile nature, she was able to lie in wait until the mother labeosaurus was distracted by another egg thief, this gave her the opportunity to dart in and snatch an egg and then run out of sight before she was even spotted. Then suddenly she heard loud trampling, when she looked behind her she found an albertosaurus, screaming and hurtling towards her looking for its next meal. Dromiceiomimus then dropped her meal and ran, she was out of sight and out of danger within seconds. Her light bones and strong muscles allowed her to run at speeds of up to fifty miles per hour.

In another part of North America, in an area which is now Wyoming, a group of troodon dinosaurs lived in the swamps, located near a river delta. The bushy forested areas of the swamps offered the troodons a safe haven from predators. Their naturally small stature, good night vision and lengthy arms allowed them to be able to creep through the underbrush and easily outrun a pursuing killer or hide in areas thick and dense with foliage where predators could not find them. But they also possessed something greater than any other animal of their time. Intelligence. With their large brain to body size ratio, their intelligence allowed them to hunt and evade much more efficiently. Hunting in packs and setting up more complex ambushes to trap potential prey. They could also evade danger through dispersing their packs when retreating from predators, forcing the pursuer to single out a single target whilst the others disappeared into the distance.

In what is now Texas, a tyrannosaurus rex was roaming the forests, searching for prey. His sensitive hearing and sense of smell had picked up familiar sounds and a known smell. The sound of rustling leaves being pulled out of bushes and deep grunting as the animal fed, the scent told him it was a large herbivorous dinosaur. He continued to move at a brisk pace, following the direction that his nose took him until the scent got so strong that he knew that his next meal was near. He slowed his pace and slowly the figure of a triceratops appeared in the distance. This was a splendid but potentially dangerous prize for him, the triceratops is one of the most heavily armoured and deadly creatures of the forest. He kept his distance, eyes locked on his target and moved to a position where he could approach his target from behind.

He moved forward towards his prey slowly, then when he was within two hundred metres he quickened his pace and charged towards the triceratops. The triceratops heard the loud footsteps coming from behind him and managed to turn around in time to face his opponent and found the tyrannosaurus just a few metres in front of him. With no time for the triceratops to charge, the tyrannosaurus caught one of the triceratops's horns with his powerful jaws and forced his head down with the triceratops's horn trapped between his teeth. Weighing up to seven tons and with a bite force of over thirteen thousand pounds, the tyrannosaurus's strength was more than a match for his armoured foe. The triceratops tried to force his head back up so he could see his enemy but only to have it forced back down again, the grip and strength of the tyrannosaurus was overwhelming. Then with one last push, the triceratops pressed hard against his foe's grip and when he felt the force coming back down, he pulled his head down in the direction it was being forced to, sending the tyrannosaur off balance. The sudden change of direction and strength from his prey caused the tyrannosaur to lose his footing, he let go by instinct and screamed as he tried to rebalance himself. But as he regained his stability, he looked to his right and saw the right horn of the triceratops coming towards him from a short distance. The movement was swift and sharp but to the eyes of the tyrannosaurus, it seemed like time had momentarily stood still. The tip of the horn came piercing through the tyrannosaur's right eye, blinding him and sending a surge of excruciating pain throughout his skull. He quickly backed away from the triceratops, keeping his distance now that the advantage has swung. He kept moving back screaming and shrieking, showing his large and sharp teeth in an attempt to intimidate the enemy.

But his horned opponent was not afraid and nor was he satisfied that the threat was over, he pointed his horns towards the tyrannosaurus and moved towards him slowly, waiting for the right moment to appear so he could make his charge. But then the triceratops felt a sharp pain in his left hind leg, as if he was caught in something and he was being dragged back. Another tyrannosaurus had caught him from behind, he was concentrating so hard on his struggle with the first tyrannosaurus that he did not notice that another was lying in wait for the right moment to strike. As the triceratops tried to turn around and face the new threat, the first tyrannosaurus saw his opportunity and quickly rushed forward and took the triceratops by the neck. The second tyrannosaurus then struck his sharp teeth into the triceratops's underbelly, piercing the flesh and causing severe bleeding. With difficulty breathing and massive blood loss, the triceratops stopped fighting and then collapsed. The two tyrannosaurus looked on and began feeding on the carcass.

In South America, in what is today Argentina. A great herd of argentinosaurus was crossing the landscape in search of new vegetation. Measuring at a size of thirty-five metres in length and weighing up to one hundred tonnes each, the great size of these beasts made the ground shake with each step they took. A group of hungry of mapusaurus looked on as the herd passed. Despite weighing up to twelve tonnes each, with powerful jaws and sharp serrated teeth, they were no match for the size and power of argentinosaurus. All they could do was watch and wait until they could single out one of the smaller, weaker and younger members of the herd.

During their time on the Earth, the dinosaurs had survived two mass extinctions, evolved and adapted to overcome almost any kind of difficulties the world could show them and ruled the Earth for over one hundred and sixty millions years. But even this great dynasty could not last forever. An asteroid eventually struck the Earth and the world changed. The climate became very different, food became scarce and most of the dinosaurs became extinct. The great dynasty of the dinosaur rule came to an end and the reason for the end of their dominance was because many of them became a victim of what made them dominant, their great size and power.

Millions of years later humans dominate the world because of their superior intelligence. Intelligence so great that they are the first species on Earth to realise the threat to life from an asteroid striking the Earth. Their intelligence has allowed them to invent and build great things. But such great achievements of mankind have also resulted in them destroying the world. Their fuel sources are now polluting the world. Their destructive weapons have resulted in them destroying each other in war. Their materialistic lifestyle derived from their intelligence to make life easier for themselves had depleted the world's natural resources. And many of their inventions and innovations has already resulted in the extinction of many other species that had in the past lived alongside them. Just like the dinosaurs, what makes humans great and powerful can also eventually destroy them. Their time for extinction may be imminent, they can if they want to, prevent or delay it, but will they?

* * *

This fable illustrates several things:

No amount of power or knowledge alone can immortalise the ongoing existence of any form of life.

Power and dominance in any form does not necessarily guarantee one would survive a great extinction, especially if that power and dominance is not used in the correct way.

32 - The Leopard and The Hyenas

It was nightfall at the African Savannah; a leopard lay on the branch of a jackal berry tree looking out into the distance, waiting patiently for the complete darkness of night. She had been resting for most of the day but the time was almost upon her to begin the hunt, for the night offers many benefits when hunting for food. The cover of darkness means that her prey cannot see her approach but her night vision allows her to see perfectly in darkness. She looked on towards the horizon, the bright red and yellow glow of the sun slowly fading and disappearing into the horizon. The leopard continued to wait and before long, the entire Savannah was covered in darkness. She rose to her feet whilst still on the branch and looked around, trying to ascertain which direction was best to find her favourite prey. It was time to hunt.

She gently climbed down the tree until she reached the ground and kept herself completely still, with her acute sense of hearing she listened for certain sounds that would tell her where she could find food. Her ears picked up the sounds of movement and rustling amongst the branches of a tree and so she began to head in that direction. After moving a kilometre from her previous position, her hearing had taken her towards a group of jackal berry trees; she could see her potential prey moving slowly among the branches. A troop of baboons was spending the night up in the safety of the branches, safe from most predators. Except the leopard. She slowly and quietly approached the trees, she knew that the baboons were swifter and more agile than her on the branches but she had one critical advantage, her night vision. She can see the baboons in the darkness but they cannot see her and with the moon temporarily covered, it was total darkness. She began to climb the trees, making as much noise as she could so that her presence was felt. She wanted to startle and scare the baboons into making the mistake of going to the ground. But today the baboons were as bold as her and many of the larger and more agile males began heading towards her position. They could not see her but could hear where she was, the other baboons kept their positions knowing the older male baboons were confronting the threat. Intimidated and confused, the leopard abandoned her hunt and left.

Later that evening, her hearing took her to a large area of open grassland. A large group of Thomson's gazelles were grazing there; prey here was plentiful for her and should be easy if she could get close enough without being heard. She slowly made her approach, not making a single sound, again the herd cannot see her in the darkness but can hear her movements if she makes any sound. This time she employs a different technique, the hunt this time will depend on her stealth. She mustn't make a single sound; otherwise the herd will be startled into a stampede. She lowered her body slightly closer to the ground, giving her a more stable stance and gently crept towards one of the gazelles. The gazelle was quietly grazing on the ground, unaware that a dangerous predator was less than fifty metres behind him and getting closer. The leopard made every step in total silence; each movement was slow and precise. Then, there was a sudden sound of a snapping branch. The herd was frightened and some of the gazelles suddenly broke into a run, the action prompted the others to do the same and soon there was a sudden stampede of movement. Thomson's gazelles could run up to fifty miles per hour and are renowned for their endurance. The leopard knew she could not hope to even keep one in her sights, catching one them will be almost impossible. She looked around her to see what it was that broke the silence during her hunt and it was not long before she spotted the hyena nearby. It had tried to shadow her movements in the hope that she could steal the leopard's prey afterwards, but her inept and awkward movements made a mockery of the hunt. The leopard knew now she had to be extra careful as she had enemies following her.

The leopard then later located a herd of roan antelope grazing in the open grassland. She picked out a large male, a target that would provide more than enough meat to last her days. Again, she relied on her stealth in the darkness and approached the large antelope in a very slow and quiet pace. This time she approached her prey from the front, moving forward each time the antelope grazed, making use of the sound of the antelope feeding to cover the sound of her movements. The grazing antelope was completely unaware of the approaching leopard. Then, when the leopard was within touching distance, she leapt forward with her jaws wide open. She pressed her teeth deep within the antelope's neck with her powerful jaws and clamped her right paw onto the antelope's back and her left paw to its underside. The rest of the herd dispersed and ran, the sound of hooves stomping heavily on the ground could be heard and the antelope struggled hard in the grasp of the leopard's teeth and claws. The leopard wrestled the antelope to the ground and kept her jaws locked on the antelope's neck, cutting off its air supply. The antelope struggled at first but became weaker and weaker with each breath due to the lack of oxygen, until eventually it stopped moving and it's breathing ceased.

Exhausted but relieved, the leopard had finally made a successful kill, but she made one critical mistake. She had miscalculated the size of the prey. This antelope was more than three times her own body weight, making it too big and heavy for her to take up a tree where she would be safe to feed. Soon, scavengers will arrive, attracted by the sound of the kill and the smell of blood. The leopard tried to feed as fast as she could, but within a few minutes, the hyena that had followed her appeared. They both fed on the carcass at first, then they struggled and tried to pull the carcass away from each other, then they fed again and then struggled again until more hyenas began to appear. The leopard looked around and knew that the situation was hopeless; she could not possibly fight off more than one hyena. With great reluctance and disappointment, she abandoned the carcass and began searching again for more prey.

* * *

When one puts greed before common sense and caution, will often find themselves losing more than what they gain.

33 - The Lone Wanderer

A soldier had been discharged from service. He had spent the last fifteen years in service of his king and country and he had served with distinction. But his dedication and loyalty had also brought him a life of conflict, pain and constant tension that had affected him in more ways than one. He decided that the one thing that had always been missing from his life that he so much wanted was peace. So it was then that he decided to dedicate himself to finding a way to live in peace, free from the stresses of conflict and chaos.

The first few years of the ex-soldier's life proved to be uneventful for him since leaving the service of the army. Despite this, it was still not the life that he had hoped for; he needed to find himself another profession now that he was no longer in the service of The King's Army. He found this difficult because he had spent much of his working life in the army and knew little else other than the arts of the military. His inability to find work made him feel disheartened, it seemed for a while his great service in the army had meant little or nothing as there was nothing for him now. He searched and looked for months until eventually he found work at the local docks, loading and unloading ships. Over time the ex-soldier grew accustomed to his new profession and he also later met someone he fell in love with whom he eventually took as his wife.

Life seemed good for the ex-soldier, his new profession did not provide a luxurious or prestigious life but it was enough for him and his wife to live a simple life of peace. But this was not to last, he soon found that his wife wanted more than just enjoying the simple things in life and as each day passed he found himself in conflict with her more and more often.

'We are not that old you and I, yet all the things we tend to do together suggest we are much older than our years,' said his wife.

'I just aim to live a peaceful life so I can leave behind me my past, age has nothing to do with it,' replied the ex-soldier.

'Life can still be peaceful even if we find other things livelier to enjoy.'

'A good meal can be lively, as is a walk around the pier and a picnic in the lush green field's if one can understand how to appreciate such things.'

'I want to learn to appreciate other things besides these.' There was a brief pause before his wife spoke again. 'Why do we not take ourselves to the tavern every so often and enjoy the fine wines and food they serve there. Or invite others around to enjoy our hospitality and company.'

'The funds that a dockworker provides are not enough to allow us to do such things. Why can't you just learn to enjoy the simple and peaceful things in life?'

'Because I am still learning to understand you.' replied his wife in a half sarcastic tone before leaving the room.

The ex-soldier found that his new employer was also beginning to show signs of becoming more challenging in his attitude towards him, from time to time he would criticise him for the quality of his work.

'You should learn to keep up with your co-workers here.' suggested his employer as he gestured his head towards other members of his staff. 'That way you will find that they will respect you more as their equal.'

'I try to work as peacefully as I can. For me a peaceful life is a productive one,' said the ex-soldier.

His employer looked at him unenthusiastically before turning and walking away.

His troubles at home also made things difficult for him in the work place, further fuelling his employer's low opinion of him. Life was gradually becoming more difficult and stressful for him as the months passed.

One day whilst he was at work his employer suddenly had an outburst of anger and directed it at him. There had been complaints from some of the captains in that it took too long for some of the ships to have their cargo unloaded. He blamed the ex-soldier for setting a bad example to the rest of his workers, for not working more competitively and thus spreading his attitude of seeking peace. The ex-soldier was angry and bitter towards his employer and felt that his presence at the dock should no longer continue. He took one last look at his employer and then walked away.

When he arrived home he found that his wife was not there and that a note had been left on the dining room table. He lit a candle and then began reading the note. The note was from his wife, in it she said that she can no longer live with him because they both want very different things and that she had tried her best to compromise but to no avail. She stated that she would not be coming back. In a fit of anger, he crushed the note in his hand and struck the candle across the room. He lowered his head and closed his eyes in dismay, then a few minutes later he smelt something burning. He looked around the room and saw that the candle which he had knocked across the room had caught the curtains and a fire had broken out. He tried to put out the flames but the fire had grown too strong and the smoke was making it hard for him to see or breathe. After a few minutes he ran out of the house to save himself. People all around were scrambling to get water and other materials to fight the flames but he just stood there in front of his own house as it burned. He thought about everything that this place represented and decided it was not worth saving.

Over the years the ex-soldier spent his life wandering endlessly from one town to the next. Using the old skills he had learnt from the military to live off the lands he walked on for food and shelter. He never saw his wife, his old house, his old employer or colleagues again and just wandered alone with no possessions. One day he came to a river, exhausted and thirsty he leant down to take a drink. He looked at his reflection and saw how he had aged and withered.

'I have no one, nowhere and nothing.' He said to himself and then laid himself down by the river. As his eyes tired and slowly closed, he thought about his life since leaving the service of The King's Army. 'All I ever wanted was to be left alone in peace. But even that seemed too much.' He reflected. Then he realised something. His life has been peaceful and he had been alone ever since he left his old house. He just never realised that he had achieved peace in his life because the peace was represented by nothing. The thought made him smile, at last he had realised his dream.

* * *

To realise what we truly have or what we have truly gained, one must look beyond what our eyes tell us.

34 - The Wind, Water, Earth and Fire

Wind, Water, Earth and Fire are the four natural elements of the world. They represent the world in many ways and are symbols of everything that exists in the world including purity, power, emotion, knowledge and wisdom.

One day each of the elements were arguing over who was the greatest of the four natural elements of the world.

'I am greater than the rest of you because I am a symbol of purity and life,' said Water.

'But what is purity without knowledge? For that is what I represent because without knowledge I can never be truly understood,' said Wind.

'No. I am greater because I am a symbol of power. For when I burn it creates the presence of what power in many forms represents. Heat, pain, intimidation… beauty.' replied Fire.

'The rest of you cannot see any further than your own thoughts. For I am greater than each and every one of you, because the earth is the mother of all living things, which is why I represent emotion. I separate what is good and evil,' said Earth.

The four of them continued to argue with one another for days but none of them were willing to concede. In the end they all agreed to hold a contest to decide. Whoever could display the most impressive show of their abilities would be declared the greatest.

The first to begin was The Wind. First he created a tornado and then another, both of them rotating violently and sucking all objects towards them before racing off at high speeds, tearing and ripping through whatever objects came into their path. Then he created several tropical cyclones over the oceans, all generating speed and power as he filled them with heat. Then he released the cyclones, each heading towards land, destroying and tearing up the coasts. The Wind then turned his attention to the sea floors, sending the energy of air through the waters, pulling the waves together into a giant spinning vortex. Such was the power and speed of the vortex that the bottom of the seabed was exposed and could be seen from the air. The others watched with admiration but were unmoved.

Next was the turn of Water. She looked on over the oceans, looking for a suitable spot to begin her work. She picked the middle of the pacific and waited and then, she forced all of the ocean's water together and lifted it up to the sky and forced it straight back down again. This resulted in a giant crown of water throwing itself back into the air, causing a circle of tidal waves several miles high racing outwards, towards all the coastal lands surrounding the pacific. The force of these waves moved entire mountains and forests.

Next the Earth shook the world so hard and with such great force that the lands and seabeds began to break and move. Two entire continents then began to move towards each other, gaining speed after each mile until they moved so fast that they both came crashing into one another. The sound of shaking earth and colliding rocks, breaking and tearing echoed throughout the entire world. Both continents were getting smaller by the day as they collided and tore through each other, breaking apart in the process until there was nothing left of either of them.

The Fire looked on, now feeling the pressure after the impressive display by the other elements. He tore open vast lands from within the world's core releasing the fire from the depths of the Earth. The world looked like it was tearing apart and liquid magma found its way to the surface and began to fill the world like a bright orange ocean. Lava also spewed into the sky continuously, forming what looked like a bright yellow and orange shower of molten rock. The sight was impressive and beautiful but also destructive.

After all this was done the elements began to argue with one another again over whose display was the most impressive but again they could not agree. They argued long and hard until eventually they decided that the contest must go on until a winner could be decided. But just as they were about to begin, they looked on the world and found that everything had already been destroyed. When they realised just how much had been lost, they knew then that their presence as the natural elements of the world was of little significance.

* * *

Such extreme vanity can lead to conflicts and conflicts can lead to the destruction of things.

35 - The Scarlet Macaw and The Cicadas

An old Scarlet Macaw was feeling depressed. He felt that his life had been wasted because he had achieved very little in his lifetime and had even failed to find himself a mate. Many of his companions and family members have gone on to do wonderful things in their lifetimes. Most have flown around the globe to see the world, flying to new places and discovering things they never knew even existed. Some grouped together during desperate times to help find new sources of food and water which contributed greatly to helping the entire community of macaws to survive. And then there were some who spent their lives interacting and communicating with other species of animals. He had even heard that one of his friends had learnt the language of humankind and spoke to humans on a regular basis.

But he had done nothing special. He never tried to see the world outside of the forest where he lived, he preferred to stay where he was and just live the life he had always known. He spent his days just roaming and flying through the forest, from tree to tree looking for different types of fruits or roaming the forest floor searching for nuts and seeds. Most of the time the food he had found was due to the hard work of other macaws who had found it first and spread the news throughout the forest. He also spent considerable time amongst the branches singing to himself and other macaws in full voice for recreation.

Now though he felt that he was living on borrowed time because of his age. He believed that it was too late for him to start over and therefore making him feel like he was even older. The last few years had made him feel weaker, he could still fly but he could not break open nuts quite as easily as he used to. His plumage was also not as bright as it used to be. The red feathers on his back were starting to whiten and the yellow and blue feathers of his wings had begun to fade. Each time he went to the river to drink, he would look into the water and see the reflection of an aging bird, he noticed that his feathers were also thinning out and some were hanging loose at the ends. His beak also looked worn from the years of nut cracking and breaking open tough fruits. He felt a lot of sadness and regret because he had lost so much time. His thoughts were that he had wasted his youth on such a trivial and insignificant life and now that he was old, it was too late to achieve anything significant.

Then one day when the Scarlet Macaw was flying through the forest in search of food and water, he noticed that the forest was different today. There was a very loud noise that filled and echoed throughout the entire forest, the sounds were long screeching and rattling calls. It was the deafening sound of mating calls of the cicada. Millions of them have come out after years of hiding underground and are now in search of a mate. The Scarlet Macaw knew because he could see that many of the trees were covered with the empty shells of cicada skins. Now that they have shed their skins, they have gone on to higher ground. The Scarlet Macaw decided to stay on the ground to search for food.

'Over here.' Cried an unfamiliar voice.

The Scarlet Macaw looked around whilst chewing on a nut to see who it was that called out but could not see anything.

'Help me.' cried out the voice again. 'I am here.'

It sounded like the sound was coming from the ground. The Scarlet Macaw then began to walk around the forest floor, searching for the source of the voice that called out to him. After walking and looking around the forest floor for several minutes, the Scarlet Macaw found who was calling out to him. He looked down onto the ground and found a male cicada with only one wing on its back, struggling to get up.

'Was that you? Did you call out to me?' asked the Scarlet Macaw.

'Yes it was. Please help me my friend, for I have fallen from the trees and I cannot get back up there as one of my wings has broken off. If I do not get myself up amongst the branches then I will not find a mate.'

The Scarlet Macaw looked upon the helpless Cicada and felt sorry for him and therefore agreed to take him up to the trees. The Cicada climbed up onto his back and the Scarlet Macaw then flew up to the trees and put the Cicada down on a branch.

'Thank you my friend. Thank you very much for your kind heart. Your good deed will not go un-rewarded, for I will tell my children one day of your noble deed,' said the Cicada.

'It was just a simple favour provided by a simple individual my friend, nothing more. Such a deed does not require a reward.' replied the Scarlet Macaw before flying away.

When the Scarlet Macaw reached the forest floor he began searching for food again until he heard another voice call out to him.

'Over here!' cried out another voice. 'Please help me.'

The Scarlet Macaw looked around again and then found a Female Cicada on the ground. 'Was that you who called out?'

'Yes sir. I cannot respond to any of the male's calls because I am having trouble clicking my wings and I do not feel strong enough to fly. Please take me up to the branches so I can respond to a mate.'

Again the Scarlet Macaw felt sorry for the Cicada and agreed to help. He took her up to the branches and set her down on a branch with a group of male cicadas.

'Thank you sir. Thank you for your kind deed, I will tell my children one day of the kindness you showed me and hope that one day you will be rewarded,' said the Cicada.

Again the Scarlet Macaw told the Cicada there was no need to thank him and he made his way back to the forest floor. By now the Scarlet Macaw was very hungry, he had not had any food for a while now but before he could go about finding food again he found another Cicada asking him for his help. Throughout the entire day the Scarlet Macaw found himself helping one Cicada after another until it was dark. By now he was too tired to look for food and decided instead to rest.

A few months had now past since the mating rituals of the Cicadas began and the Scarlet Macaw was again foraging the forest floor for food. As he was looking he heard loud noises coming down from the trees. He looked up and found millions of newly born cicadas coming down towards him.

'It's him!' cried the Cicadas. 'He is the old bird with the fading feathers who helped our parents.'

'Who are you?' asked the Scarlet Macaw.

'Wasn't it you who helped our parents get to the trees?'

'Well yes, I did help some cicadas get up to the trees a few months ago.'

'Our parents have told us about you. You helped them when they called out to you. If it was not for you sir, then many of us would not be here today.'

As the Cicadas came down from the tree trunks, some of them were carrying fruits and nuts. They all walked towards the Scarlet Macaw and surrounded him, placing the food on the ground into piles.

The Scarlet Macaw looked on. He had never seen so much food in his life and in such a variety. 'Thank you my friends. I did not realise what I did made so much difference to so many.'

'That is what makes your deed all the greater. You did not realise how important it was and you still went on and did it. Our parents told us that if we are to see you we must reward you for your kindness,' said the Cicadas as they laid down even more fruits and nuts for the Scarlet Macaw.

The Scarlet Macaw looked on with astonishment. It all reminded him of back in his youth, when he used to hear all sorts of stories about the wonderful things his companions and members of his family had done. He now finally felt like he was one of them.

* * *

When we have made mistakes or bad choices in the past and feel that we no longer have the time to start over then we know that we have grown old. But if we can help others to achieve their goals, it can give us a new sense of youth because by doing so dispels the common belief that with old age comes uselessness.

36 - The Beavers and The Dormouse

A family of beavers were busy working. They were building dams to divert water to a favourable area for them to form an artificial lake. They were also collecting branches, leaves and grasses to build a lodge in the middle of that lake that can only be entered from under water. Food was also being stockpiled as they gathered logs, branches and other forms of vegetation that they placed in an area under the water of the artificial lake.

The dormouse looked on in fascination, wondering why the beavers were working so hard and persistently. He approached one of the beavers to ask.

'Why do you all work so hard?' asked the Dormouse.

'We are preparing for winter my friend. It is not far away now and we must ensure that we have enough food to last the cold months ahead.'

'I see. But why the dams and that large looking hideout in the middle of the lake?'

'That hideout is our lodge, we live there during the winter and in the summer we use it as a safe haven to protect ourselves from enemies which is why it can only be entered from under the water. The dams as you can see is to create this lake, with this much water we can move around faster and easier and the lake also helps us to store food for the winter.' The Beaver pointed his head to an area of the lake where one of the other beavers had placed a branch under the water. 'You see there? Where a member of my family has just placed a branch under the water? That is our storage area where we keep our winter food. The cold water during winter helps keep the food fresh for us during the winter months.'

'But all this work my friend. Why do you even bother? Isn't it easier to simply hibernate during the winter and then come back out when the weather is more favourable?'

'Of course it is. But we like to spend our winters doing better things other than just sleep.'

'What else is there to do in winter? It is so cold and unpleasant.'

'Have you ever been outside during the winter my friend?'

'No. Like I say it is too cold.'

'Well if you do manage to come out during the winter it is actually quite pleasant in many ways. Yes of course it is cold, but it is also quiet and peaceful. This means we can move around on land more freely and with so many others hibernating, we don't have to worry about predators as much. This gives us the freedom to see and visit areas we don't normally venture out to. My children also like to play in the snow and some evenings we can invite friends over for a social gathering or any kind of festivity that we enjoy. This can only be possible if we complete what we are doing right now.'

The Dormouse felt inspired and excited by what the beaver told him. He too wanted to be able to visit these places he had never seen, play in the snow and be able to get together with friends during the winter for some revelry. He thanked the Beaver for sharing with him such useful information and then went about to make his own preparations for the winter.

First the Dormouse gathered some branches and leaves for new bedding but then fell asleep shortly after returning to his nest. When he awoke the next day, he continued with his new venture but found himself falling asleep again after a short period of work. Then when he was awake again he tried to continue with his work but found himself eating nuts and berries and then went back to his nest to sleep. Each time he worked, he just ended up sleeping again after a short while until eventually, winter came and the Dormouse had no choice but to hibernate for the winter. He had failed to complete his task of preparing for winter.

Meanwhile the beavers were enjoying the winter in their lodge. They had completed the building of their dams, reinforced their lodge to ensure themselves a safe place to spend the winter and stockpiled enough food to help them through the cold months ahead. They were now feasting with friends they had invited over and the next day they ventured outside and enjoyed the peaceful surroundings that the winter brought. The children also enjoyed playing in the snow, safe from potential predators.

* * *

If we can complete what we do today, then we can plan for greater things tomorrow.

37 - The Hermit Crab and The Sea Anemone

A Hermit Crab was out looking for food one day and his sense of smell had taken him to the rotting carcass of a dead fish and he began feeding on it with his claws. Unknown to him, an octopus was watching close by. The octopus waited until he was busy feeding before he approached. Being a very messy eater, the Hermit Crab quickly made a mess of his meal and scraps of fish started to flow around him, little did he realise that he was giving the octopus the signal to attack. In his haste however, the octopus made the mistake of mistiming his attack and could only manage to get two of his tentacles onto the Hermit Crab. Thus he was unable to suck in the Hermit Crab quickly and at the same time alerting the Hermit Crab of his presence. The Hermit Crab instinctively responded by clasping his powerful claws into one of the Octopus's tentacles. Feeling the pain from the power of the Hermit Crab's claws, the Octopus desperately tried to shake him off his tentacle. The Hermit Crab held on for a few more seconds to ensure that the octopus would be in too much pain to continue the attack after he let go. When he finally let go, the Hermit Crab found himself flung towards a nearby rock and he immediately crawled under it for safety.

After his close encounter with the octopus the other day, the Hermit Crab decided that he would need help in future to fend off potential enemies. As he walked along the seabed he spotted an Anemone clinging to a rock. The Hermit Crab approached it and tapped the Anemone on its side with his claw.

'What do you want from me?' asked The Anemone.

'Climb onto my shell and it will be your new home,' said the Hermit Crab.

'Why would I want to live on your shell? I am happy here and have no need to follow a hermit.'

'You will be better off if you come with me. If you live one my shell, I can take you to places where you can find fresh plankton and I will also share with you any food I find on my travels.'

'But why do you want me to come with you?'

'You can help protect me. The toxins from your powerful sting will help ward off predators such as the octopus, so by coming together we can help each other.'

The Anemone thought about what the Hermit Crab said and eventually agreed. She climbed onto his back and the Hermit Crab was happy that he can now search for food without having to be on the lookout for danger and the Anemone looked forward to having a regular supply of food being provided for her.

Over the next few months, the new partnership between the Hermit Crab and the Anemone was successful. There was not a single day that went by where the Anemone had to go hungry and each time an octopus attacked the Hermit Crab, it found itself being painfully stung by the Anemone's tentacles. Over time the two of them became good friends, as they knew they could always rely on each other. But then one day the Anemone started to think about her friend's dependence on her.

'It is probably best that you remember and practice how to defend yourself without me. For I may not always be able to protect you,' said the Anemone.

'But why? Are you thinking of leaving me? I thought you were happy here.'

'I am happy my friend. I just worry for you because I seem to be your only method of defence and you cannot rely on me forever, for one day I may not be here on your shell or I may not be able to fend off the next octopus.'

'Well you just told me that you won't be leaving me and why wouldn't you fend off an octopus for me?'

'It is not that I wouldn't defend you my friend but there may be times when I can't.'

The Hermit Crab ignored what the Anemone said and decided not to worry. For there has never been an octopus she could not fend off and therefore he gave it no further thought.

Then one day the Anemone fell severely ill and was not able to tell the Hermit Crab who was busy feeding on a sea snail he had just found. Due to this distraction and the Anemone being ill neither of them were able to spot the Octopus behind them. The Octopus struck with precision and engulfed both the Hermit Crab and the Anemone straight into its mouth. Due to the Anemone's illness, she was not able to sting the octopus and because the Hermit Crab had been completely ignorant of his surroundings they both found themselves devoured.

* * *

When one becomes too dependent on others or too dependent on assistance from external sources, they will often forget how to depend on themselves.

38 - The Rat and The Cockroaches

A Rat climbed out of a drain from the sewers in search of a new home. He looked around his surroundings and found himself in the middle of an urban street. It was late in the night and the streets were relatively quiet but there were still people who could be seen walking along the pavements. Every so often, someone would come out of a dark corner or come out of a door from the many buildings that lined the streets. The odd vehicle could be seen driving past every few minutes, although many parts of the area were very dark, the roads were lit up by the street lights, forming a track of light wherever the roads went.

The Rat moved along the roads and pavements cautiously, being careful not to be seen. He would move a few metres and then stop to make use of something in his surroundings to cover himself from potential danger, like hiding behind a bush or under a street bench. When he was certain that the area around him was clear, he would move on. He did not know where to go only that he had to keep moving because where he was now provided no shelter or food for him and therefore he must find a more beneficial place to live. The Rat suddenly heard the sound of a door opening nearby and quickly ran towards a large post box and hid himself behind it. He heard footsteps moving towards him, the sounds got louder for a moment but then gradually grew quieter as he waited, until the sound was gone and the Rat continued on his uncertain journey.

After wandering around the streets and hiding in various places, the Rat came across a quiet house. All the lights in the building were turned off and the Rat noticed that the bottom right corner of the front door was damaged. He jolted his head up and down to get a better look before moving forward quickly a few paces. As he got closer to the front door of the house, he noticed that the damage had left a rough triangular shaped hole in the bottom right corner of the door. He realised now that this house could offer him shelter and there was an easy way in for him. He ran as quickly as he could towards the steps of the porch and climbed with all the remaining strength he had until he reached the top and then headed straight towards the hole in the corner of the door.

It was dark but slightly warmer inside the house. The Rat was hungry but he was also very tired from his long journey and wanted to rest. He kept walking in the direction that his senses told him to go, whichever direction he could feel the warmth coming from he would follow until he came to a door. He began chewing into the corner of the door until there was a small hole, large enough for him to fit through. He found himself inside the boiler cupboard and the extra warmth inside it was soothing, he laid himself down and quickly drifted off to sleep.

The next day the Rat explored the house that he had spent the night in. At first he could not see any human occupants and everywhere he looked there were objects and debris spread across the floors. He stopped and inspected each object he came across, sniffing and chewing on various bits of debris, searching for something edible. He walked straight down the corridor from the right of the boiler cupboard he had just come out of and came to the living room of the house. Just to the left of the entrance to the living was a staircase leading to the upstairs, which the Rat ignored for now. Inside the living room was a single table, a few chairs and a sofa. All the furniture looked badly worn and discoloured. The floor was uncarpeted and like the rest of the house was littered with rubbish, to the far right of the living room was the kitchen area. A window just in front of the kitchen sink was open.

The Rat made his way towards the kitchen and here he found what he had been looking for. His sense of smell already told him there was food there and when he reached the kitchen area he found the floor to be covered with all sorts of edibles. Splashes and morsels of various substances, pieces of meat, cereal flakes and plastic wrappers with bits of food still inside them were strewn across the kitchen floor. The Rat began feeding ravenously starting with whichever piece of food he could get to first. As he was feeding, he noticed something had flown in from the window and landed on the floor. When he looked at it he saw it move, it was brown in colour and had wings, antennae and six legs. It was a cockroach. As it walked around, the Rat noticed him feeding as well and soon more of them arrived through the window, but The Rat ignored it as there was plenty of food all over the floor. The Rat moved a few inches every few minutes, taking a few bites from each morsel before moving on to the next. Then there was an unexpected sound, the sound of something heavy and moving, the Rat looked around to see if he could see where the source of the sound was coming from. As he looked the sound slowly got louder, like something heavy thumping the ground at a slow but constant pace. The Rat located the source of the sound and saw something coming down from the staircase, it looked like the house had another occupant and its feet were coming down from the top of the stairs. The Rat felt startled and quickly ran towards the couch in the centre of the living room, he hid under the couch and kept himself almost completely still in the dark gloomy space. Then, he heard and saw something coming towards him. It was one of the cockroaches.

'Don't worry. He is harmless; he does not mind our company. Most of the time he completely ignores us. He also leaves lots of food lying around for us as you already seen,' said the Cockroach.

The Cockroach and The Rat looked up towards the ceiling above them, which suddenly came spreading downwards, behind them in the space outside of the couch they could see two feet resting on the floor.

'Do you think he would react badly if he saw me?' asked the Rat.

'As long as you stay out of his way and don't provoke him then I don't see why he would.'

'How long have you been here?'

'I have been coming to this house for food and shelter for long time now. Just don't stay too long, there are more and better places out there and nothing lasts forever.'

Before the Rat could ask the Cockroach what he meant by that, he noticed the ceiling above him flattening out again. The feet that rested on the floor began to walk away. The Rat crept out from under the couch and looked around. When he was certain there was no one else around he quickly ran back to the boiler room where he spent the night.

Over the next few days the Rat felt very much settled in his new home. It provided him with adequate shelter and enough food on a daily basis. He also met the human occupant of the house on many occasions and although at first he showed signs of disdain towards the Rat, he eventually got use to him and showed little concern whenever the Rat appeared.

Several months had now passed and the Rat noticed that he no longer saw his human counterpart and wondered what had happened to him. The nights tended to be darker than it used to be and food was slowly running out. Early one morning the Rat was in the kitchen, searching for what little food was left in there, a single cockroach was there with him.

'I think it is almost to leave now,' said the Cockroach.

'Where are you going?' asked the Rat.

'I am going to look for another house to live in. another source of food and shelter.'

'You are not going to return?'

'There is nothing left here and nothing to stay for. If you do not leave, this place will eventually leave you.'

The Rat thought to himself for moment and gave a look of confusion. 'My friend I believe you are confused, the land beneath our feet cannot just move and even if it does it cannot move very far.'

'Give it time and you will see. Haven't you noticed that although things still seem adequate, it is not getting any better and is in fact slowly getting worse? You should leave this place soon.'

The Rat ignored what the cockroach said and continued in his search for food.

As the days continued to pass, the Rat found that food was becoming harder and harder to find. He also noticed that each room in the house had become colder since the disappearance of his co-occupant and the nights were significantly darker. One morning the Rat was sleeping in the boiler room, until suddenly he was awoken by a loud sound. The sound was like that of heavy solid materials colliding against one another and he also noticed that the room was shaking slightly. He ran out of the boiler room to find a safer place to rest but found that every room and area in the house was shaking loudly. His only instinct now was to leave and he ran out of the house. When he got outside, he saw that the house was surrounded by people and machinery and they were tearing it down. The Rat realised now that he had no choice, the house was gone and the time has come for him to leave.

* * *

One must learn to walk away and move on from a situation when things become precarious. For if we do not walk away from the situation, we could find that the situation will walk away from us.

39 - The Leopard and The Baboon

It was late afternoon and a troop of baboons were by the river quenching their thirst and resting in the comfort of the afternoon breeze. The Savannah was beginning to cool as the sun was ready to set and the baboons looked on in anticipation as the time was nearing for them to take to the safety of the trees. It would not be long now until nightfall, a time when predators like lions, hyenas and leopards would be most active in their hunting and baboons would be potential prey. It was time for the troop to be on their way home and the Alpha Male signalled to the rest of the troop to start moving back to the safety of the acacia trees, a few miles north of their current location.

Many members of the troop began moving; others took one last mouthful of water from the river before turning and making their way back home. It would be their last drink until sunrise the next day. Females took hold of their young who clung to their bellies as they moved; others simply hopped onto their mother or father's backs as they began moving. Other animals were also moving away. Impalas, mongoose and zebras who normally band together with the baboons during the day were beginning to disperse from the crowd. They were now going their own separate ways, looking for a safe haven for the night.

The long march home began at a steady pace, the Alpha Male lead from the front, staying vigilant on his lookout for trouble. Every ten to fifteen steps he would stop and look around, making sure that all members of the troop kept moving and that there was nothing else in the distance, like lions or leopards lying in wait for an ambush. As he looked around he spotted a member of his troop whom he was familiar with for the wrong reasons. He spotted him walking in the centre of the troop, surrounded by other baboons, some of whom were old and vulnerable.

'YOU! THE RUNNER! OVER HERE!' Shouted the Alpha Male as he stood whilst the others slowly passed him. He waited for The Runner to approach him.

The Runner knew that the alpha male was not fond of him and always tried to keep his distance, he was not looking forward to this encounter. He stopped a few paces before the Alpha Male. 'What is it?'

'I was thinking. As you are such a good runner, you should go on ahead as a lookout. If there is danger, you will be the first to know and with the way you run, the rest of us will know about it soon enough.' The Alpha Male stared at The Runner. He remembered the previous night's incident; where a lone lioness attacked the troop. She should have been spotted in time but the sentry was missing. The sentry on guard was The Runner but during the attack he was nowhere to be seen and as a consequence the troop lost a healthy member of their group. A few hours after the attack, The Runner was seen running back to his post, everyone suspected that he spotted the lioness but instead of alerting the troop, he ran away to save himself. That was how he earned himself the name, The Runner.

'I will not disappoint you.' The Runner quickly replied and was immediately on his way.

The troop carried on their journey; the Alpha Male kept his attention in the distance and told the others to do the same. Then, he noticed everyone looking in the same direction, a small cloud of dust was approaching and without warning there were screams throughout the area and many baboons began to run. The Runner was returning with a lone lion close behind him. The Runner changed direction frequently as he ran, darting left and right, trying to throw the lion off balance and slow him down but when he realised the troop was nearby he then ran straight towards them. The Runner ran straight towards the centre of where the troop were all standing, straight towards the older and more vulnerable members of the troop. The Runner turned just a few paces from where the elderly baboons were. The lion noticed that they were slow to respond and instead of continuing his chase for The Runner he carried straight on and took one of the elderly baboons by the neck. The lion swung the elderly baboon across to his right whilst clasped in his powerful jaws and then pressed him down to the ground breaking the elderly baboon's neck. The lion then left the area, taking his prize with him, the troop waited until he was out of sight before re-assembling together again.

The Alpha Male angrily ran through the ranks of every member of the troop, looking for The Runner but he was nowhere to be seen. 'Where is he?' He shouted, as he looked around frantically. He searched again for a moment but then realised that the troop could still be in danger unless they find a safe place to spend the night. Reluctantly, he ordered the troop to continue their march.

The troop arrived home amongst the acacia trees just before nightfall and began climbing to get themselves to the safety of the branches. The baboons all felt safe up in the trees for they knew that most predators would not be able to climb high enough or at all to reach them, except for the leopard. With perfect night vision and the ability climb as well as they could, the leopard was a deadly foe, the troop therefore was vigilant throughout the night and placed two sentries on guard.

Shortly after nightfall, The Runner had finally managed to catch up with his troop. He approached the trees cautiously as he had no doubt that the Alpha Male and many other members of his troop were still angry and bitter towards him. Just as he was about to climb up one of the trees where his clan was resting, he heard some unusual sounds. It sounded like something was slowly approaching the trees from the ground. It was unusual enough for members of the troop to be moving on the ground at this time and the sounds of movement were too subtle and soft to be made by baboons. Then, he picked up the scent, as the sounds grew closer, he felt fearful, it is definitely not another baboon. His instincts told him that it must be another lion or a leopard as very few other animals would be active at this time. He tried to deduce which direction the sounds were coming from and when he did, he thought about warning the troop but then felt that he could use the troop to distract the intruder for him whilst he escapes. He turned and ran.

The Runner returned to the troop later that night and found it in a state of shock. They were attacked by a leopard who managed to get up to the branches without being detected by the sentries and attacked and killed an adult female. The troop did not see and barely heard the attack until the leopard was gone and stayed in a state of panic long after the incident, not knowing if the danger had passed. The Runner found himself able to interact with the rest of the troop again. Now that another incident had shaken the troop and he was not the one to blame for it, or at least nobody thought he was. The attention had now shifted to the two baboons who were supposed to be on sentry duty.

The Runner felt no guilt or remorse and even looked at himself with a sense of pride. 'I am too clever for this troop. I have outwitted them and a leopard.' He thought to himself as he lay down on a branch and drifted off to sleep.

The next evening the leopard returned and attacked the troop again. This time the sentries detected him and alerted the rest of the baboons, the screams of the troop were now in full voice. The Runner kept himself alert, trying to identify the position of where the leopard was, and then suddenly, the commotion grew louder on one of the trees. The Runner knew now that the leopard was amongst one of the other trees and decided it was a good time to make his escape. He made his way to the ground and ran as fast as he could.

Over the next few months the same leopard would attack the troop a further five times and each time he would carry away a dead baboon. Each time the leopard attacked, The Runner would run away from the situation instead of standing strong and helping the rest of the troop defend themselves. Then, one night when the leopard attacked again, The Runner as usual ran away the moment he knew that the leopard had come back to attack, but unknown to him the troop was prepared this time. The troop sensed the leopard's presence before he was within reaching distance of the trees, the screams of every baboon was now in full voice and within seconds the entire troop was alerted to the danger. The males all positioned themselves into strategic positions, readying themselves to encircle and ambush the leopard wherever he attacked. Each tree the leopard climbed he found himself faced with a group of large angry adult males standing ready to attack. Feeling intimidated he tried another tree, trying to find one where he could isolate a single baboon from the rest of the troop but each time he tried it was the same. He tried to catch some of the baboons by surprise and jumped from one tree to the next, only to find himself surrounded again from all sides. Eventually, the leopard gave up and decided to leave in search of easier prey.

A few hours later The Runner was making his way home. He assumed that the leopard had already killed another member of his troop and had left to enjoy his next meal. He was making his way back to the troop with a carefree attitude, believing there would be no trouble on the way. He then passed a large rock that was familiar to him, he knew he was close to home now because this rock was the first object he passed when he ran away to safety. Then suddenly, he felt a heavy weight falling upon him and heard a loud roar, his entire body felt like it was being crushed towards the ground and sharp objects were piercing into his arm, shoulder and neck. The leopard that attacked the troop earlier had picked up his trail and scent. The Runner failed to spot him hiding behind the rock due the darkness and his lack of caution whilst making his way home. The Runner felt his breathing slowly fail, until eventually he could breathe no more and the darkness became complete.

* * *

If you will not fight for your home then there would be nowhere for you to go.

40 - The Librarian, The Soldier and The Poet

There was once a soldier who had served many years in the military. His colleagues had always known him for being a brave man but with a short temperament. His tendency to lose his judgement from time to time has led him to unnecessary confrontations with his adversaries, superiors and colleagues. But, at times this trait had also served him well not only in his duties but also in his daily life, he was not afraid to make aggressive decisions because he felt that this helped him to get things done. As far as he was concerned, he saw his temperament as an asset.

After leaving the military, the ex-soldier had found himself a new job as a security guard for a private club. The club owner felt that having an ex-soldier could help tighten security and soon enough the ex-soldier proved to be a valued member of his staff. He was always punctual and turned up for work on time, he followed every procedure exactly how his superiors had laid out and was always vigilant in his work. Then one night the club was much busier than usual and access had to be limited. When it was announced that the club was full and that no one else can be granted entrance, a man came out from the middle of the queue and jumped all the way to the front.

'Hey!' The man shouted at the ex-soldier as he was looking away. 'You have to let me in. I am good friends with the owner here and I come on a regular basis.' The man was abrasive in his attitude.

The ex-soldier stared at him for a minute before answering. 'No. You cannot enter and I don't care who you are and what you do.'

The man grinned at the ex-soldier. 'If this was a comedy club then I would advise you to say that more often, it would be good for business. Your customers will know that even the doorman is funny.' The man then tried to push his way passed him.

The ex-soldier waited for a moment and then suddenly turned around and grabbed the man by the shoulders. The man's attitude and words had caused him to lose his judgement and he did not realise what he was doing even as he turned the man around to face him and then hurled him against the wall before grabbing him by the throat and arm. 'HOW FUNNY IS THIS?" Shouted the ex-soldier and then pulled the man towards him before slamming his head against the wall. He raised his fist to strike at the man but then felt several bodies surrounding him, pulling him away.

It took a few minutes before the ex-soldier was calm again. It was only now, as he looked around himself that he noticed the commotion he had caused. The customers waiting in the queue were staring at him nervously and spoke amongst themselves and the man he had assaulted was speaking to one of his colleagues as they waited for the manager to arrive. The ex-soldier tried to subconsciously keep his distance and kept his eyes averted from anyone else.

'I'm afraid I have to let you go. With immediate effect.' A voice called out.

The ex-soldier turned around and found his manager looking at him in the eye, his face was calm but his cold stare made it obvious he was angry. The ex-soldier looked at him briefly before looking down and then left.

She scanned the barcode on the individual's membership card and checked his account for any outstanding fines or late returns. There were none. 'This book has been signed out to you for a week sir, please ensure it is returned within seven days,' said the librarian.

The library member took the book from her gently and smiled. 'Will do.' The man then turned away and left.

The librarian valued her job and her way of life. Not because it brought her wealth or because it gave her recognition but simply because it helped keep her life peaceful. Like many of the working class, she spent most of her time at work, her job did not bring much financial reward but enough to sustain her. With it she could support herself, enjoy the simple things in life and more importantly, it helped and taught her to stay away from confrontations.

It was the end of the day now and the librarian was getting ready to leave her place of work. She picked up her bag from under the circular front desk that surrounded her and then walk over to the parting gap where she entered from earlier. A senior colleague was waiting for her by the front entrance and pressed the button to open the automatic doors as she approached. She found the day still bright and calm as she stepped out and made her way into town towards the seaside, she felt that it was a good time to take a stroll. The beach was almost empty and was silent of human activity, as she walked along the coast she listened to the soft sounds of the waves, water moving at a calm pace. Her hair flowing gently behind her with the cool breeze as she walked, feeling the soft touch of the sand beneath her feet and the odd cry of the seagulls as she walked at her leisurely pace. The feeling was of calm and peace and she could not help but close her eyes for a few seconds to enhance the feeling of her other senses by shutting off her eyes for a few moments.

'I hear waves, flow soothingly and I appreciate it.' She thought to herself. Her mind was clear for a few seconds before her thoughts were active again. 'The skies are calm and I can relax under it. The ground is soft and I take comfort in it. Such peace undisturbed, I revel in it.'

The next day the librarian was back at work. A man approached the front desk with a large book titled War and Art and asked for it to be taken out but just as the librarian was about to scan the barcode, another man approached the desk and intervened. The second man argued that he wanted that book and that he had come into possession of it before the first man who approached. The first man dismissed his claim and stated that he found the book unattended on one of the work desks. Then the second man argued that it was he who had left it on the desk whilst he went to look for another book. The argument between the two men became increasingly heated and seemed like it was about to erupt.

'Excuse me?' interrupted the librarian. 'We do have other books of a similar subject available. Why don't you have a look at them sir and see if they are to your liking and I will make sure you can keep it for an extra week if you wish to do so. In the meantime, I will reserve this book for you so you can have it the next time it is in,' she said to the second man.

The second man looked at the librarian for a moment, then looked at the first man and reluctantly agreed. The librarian then explained to him where he could locate the books she recommended and he then made his way to the area of the library where those books were kept. The librarian then scanned the book for the first man and as he took the book from her, he thanked her many times for her constructive and noble deed and even offered to give a donation to the library.

Later that night, the librarian was at home thinking of the events that took place at work that day. She thought deeply about what caused the events between the two men, how it was resolved and how it made each of them feel afterwards. 'I find people can compromise, I am grateful for it. Not always are they fair but I understand it. People can give anything, if we see the virtue in it. Benevolence can be noticed; I am pleased to know it.' She thought to herself and then paused for a moment and then began thinking again. 'To have peace in life is to realise it. To not have peace is to be distracted from it. To achieve peace is to value it. Such is life, I savour it.' The librarian began to realise how her own thoughts and experiences had triggered something creative in her, something she never realised she could achieve. She then began to write down her thoughts and constructed them into a poem.

Over the months, the librarian kept thinking about her general life experiences and her appreciation for peace at a deeper level and each time she would write down her thoughts. This lead to her writing more and more poems and eventually she published her work and became a successful poet.

* * *

Those who value peace over conflict will find it easier to achieve more in their lifetime.

41 - The Thief and The Blind Woman

There was once a man who lived his life by being a thief. He never tried to live an honest life, he always felt that working for a living was too difficult and it was much easier to steal and deceive. He did not know or understand how to do anything else other than stealing. He never tried to learn a trade because he was afraid of failure and he refused to do manual labour because he could not tolerate the fatigue. Stealing though, it was easy. All that was required for him was to know how the system and the people he was stealing from worked. He would seize items and goods from those he knew were vulnerable. The elderly and infirm who could not fight back, the foolish and naive who lacked the wits to be vigilant and the unaware and distracted who knew no better.

One day he followed a woman into town, he knew where she was going for he had been keeping a watchful eye over her for days. When they reached town the woman went straight over to a local jewellery store and greeted the owner of the store with a joyful attitude. The Thief knew she had a close friendship with the owner of the store and this could provide him with an opportunity. He entered the store shortly after the woman entered and pretended he was looking around at the various jewellery on display. It was a relatively small store with a single room for customer entry, with floor space enough for just under ten people, waist high open wooden counters were placed on the left and right sides of the store filled with various jewellery, and at the back was a slightly larger counter where the store keeper stood behind. The Thief went straight towards the back of the store where the storeowner was busy talking to the woman whom he followed. He tried to avoid suspicion by making himself look like a genuine customer, placing himself where everyone could clearly see him. He kept his eyes on the jewellery displayed on the countertop where the storeowner was standing behind whilst talking to her friend, he admired the many expensive necklaces on display.

'I am having trouble at home with my husband,' said the woman to the storeowner.

This was the moment the Thief had been waiting for, the storeowner being in deep conversation with the woman he followed. 'Do you sell any bracelets?' He asked the storeowner.

The storeowner suddenly turned her attention to the thief with little care. 'Uh yes. They are over there,' said the storeowner gesturing her hand towards the wooden counter on the far right of the store. 'Please. Take a look.' The storeowner then quickly turned her attention back to her friend with a look of concern on her face. 'What is it?'

The Thief casually walked over to the location indicated by the storeowner whilst she and her friend stood in the corner of the other side of the store. He looked briefly over the counter and then picked a bracelet at random and placed it under his clothing. He looked behind him and found the storeowner still in deep conversation with her friend and then casually left the store. As he walked in the streets he noticed a blind man walking with a cane and followed him. When he was confident that there was no one else around he quickly walked up to the blind man and tripped him. As the blind man was struggling to get himself back up, the Thief quickly snatched his purse and ran.

A few days had now passed since he stole the bracelet from the jewellery store and the purse from the blind man. The Thief wondered the streets in town, searching for his next target. Although he had gained a sizeable profit from his recent exploits, his instincts made him continue, stealing was his full time profession and today he was late for work. After walking for a few minutes he found himself in the town square, it was quiet in the square today and he could only see one other person. A woman in a dark purple dress was walking alone with her right hand held out in front of her as if she was trying to reach out and push something directly in front of her. Suddenly the woman tripped and fell, the Thief ran towards her and helped her up.

'Are you alright?' Asked the Thief.

The Woman did not even look at him after he spoke and concentrated on getting herself back up from the floor. She patted her dress with her hands at random places without even looking at what she was doing. 'Thank you,' she said, her eyes meanwhile were fixated away from the Thief, he was standing right next to her on her left but she looked directly ahead.

Her dress was of a very casual style but the Thief could feel the smoothness and high quality of the material that it was made of, it was no doubt expensive. The Thief looked at her in the face and then waved his hand out in front of her to which she did not respond. 'You're blind?' He asked.

'Yes. I was with one of my servants but I somehow lost her which is why I am alone now.' The woman raised her left hand to her temple and brushed her hair back as if to neaten it.

The Thief looked at her hand and noticed she wore a thick gold ring, studded with rubies. He looked at her ring like it was the most beautiful object in the world, his eyes following it even as she lowered her hand. He kept staring at the ring and looked like he had been hypnotised and held in a trance.

'Do you mind having a bit of company for a while?' The Woman asked.

It took a few moments for the Thief to come to his senses. 'No. Of course not.'

The two of them walked around the town square together and engaged in deep conversation until the woman's servant had found her.

'I am really sorry mistress,' said the servant bowing her head in front of her as if in an act of submission. 'I stopped to help someone and before I knew it you were gone.'

'It's all right Julia. Luckily I was found by this kind man who kept me safe,' said the Blind Woman.

'Thank you sir. Thank you so much for looking after my mistress,' said the servant.

'Will I see you again?' asked the Thief.

The woman thought for a few moments before speaking. 'Yes. I am sure we will be in the company of each other again. I come here to the square often, you will find me here again.'

'I look forward to seeing you again soon,' said the Thief.

'I hope so too. Come Julia, it is time for us to go home.'

Over the next few weeks the Thief met up with the Blind Woman many times and they spent much time together. As he suspected, the Blind Woman was in possession of great wealth and she was of noble birth. He found out that she enjoyed going out for walks, dining out and she also enjoyed theatre because it allowed her to immerse herself with the world around her and at the same time enjoy the recreational values of these activities. However, whenever the Blind Woman tried to find out more about the Thief, he would either lie or change the subject.

At first the Thief tried to win her trust to get close to her and therefore putting himself in a position to obtain her riches. They spent time together dining at expensive inns and attending operas, to begin with he always insisted that he should pay but soon the Blind Woman would find herself paying for everything. The Thief would eventually avoid paying for anything by deliberately forgetting his purse or by telling the blind woman that he was having financially difficulty.

One day the Thief met up with the blind woman again at the square. Her servant was there with her as she always was.

The Thief greeted her by gently taking hold of her hands. 'It's good to see you again. You're looking as radiant as always,' he said.

The Blind Woman stayed silent and then pulled her hands away from him. 'Julia. Bring the purse,' she said to her servant.

Her servant approached the Thief, her face displayed an obvious disdain for him and then handed him a small pouch.

'This is what you been after for some time isn't it? Money?' asked the Blind Woman. There was a moment of silence before she spoke again. 'I have also been told you have been paying a lot of attention to this.' The Blind Woman took off her gold ring studded with rubies and then tossed it to the floor. It landed next to the Thief's left foot. 'You're probably wondering how I know. Well, you always seemed very secretive about yourself and never told me what you do. You have extravagant tastes but you're never willing to pay for anything. My servants have also informed me that you are a thief and they have witnessed some of your exploits. You can take what you want now and I will not report you to the authorities. And if you must know, I am doing this because I feel sorry for a man like you who is willing to deceive a blind person just for coin. Just tell me. Can you promise never to do this again to anyone else or try to change your ways?'

The Thief tried to think of something to say but did not know how to respond. There was nothing left for him to lose now, he had got what he came for and there was no threat of the Blind Woman having him arrested for what she knows about him. He could simply tell the truth that he is a thief by choice because he refuses to learn any other trade. But he couldn't. The Thief picked up the ring from the ground and then walked away, never looking back as shame and humiliation gripped him in that he had been exposed and his gains were out of charity and pity.

* * *

When there is nothing left to lose and one still refuses to respond, defend themselves or face the truth, only then can one be certain that they are a coward.

42 - The School of Fish

A Juvenile Bluefin Tuna and three of his friends had just entered the open ocean of the Atlantic. It has been just over a year since they all hatched in their spawning area in the Mediterranean Sea and now they have come of age to enter their new home. The open ocean looked the same but different to them, near the water's surface the ocean could sometimes look like an endless vacuum of bright blue water with rays of white light shining through the surface. Other times it could look like a battlefield, with scores of different marine life competing for food.

A school of mackerel were swimming together in unison and changing direction together every few seconds as a pod of dolphins and some sea lions charged them, each time snatching a fish in their jaws. Even birds dived down, taking wing under water to grab a mackerel with their beaks. When the bluefin tunas spotted this feeding frenzy, they all quickly joined in, darting into the school of mackerel in all directions. Then, there were suddenly hundreds of bluefins everywhere, all desperate to join in and snatch a fish. As everyone was distracted by the mass feeding fury, some great white sharks had appeared in the distance and were approaching the feeding area at speed. One of the sharks isolated and picked out a dolphin from its pod, then another caught one of the bluefins as it darted out of the school of mackerel. The Juvenile Bluefin looked on as he realised that the shark had caught one of his friends, he and his two remaining friends then left the area after realising the danger.

The Juvenile Bluefin found the ocean floor was very different in appearance compared to the area near the surface, as he and his friends swam close to the bottom. Much of the ocean floor was covered with rocks and corals like a series of miniature escarpments and cliffs, with small spaces of white sandy floors lying between them like canyons and gorges. Various fish swam between the corals and moray eels dashing out of crevices trying to grab a fish with its sharp teeth. Brain Corals, shaped like a large human brain, lay amongst various other corals such as the staghorn and elkhorn that grew out in branches shaped liked the horns of a stag. Starfish and anemones clung on to the rocks, ghost crabs crawled along the ocean floor scavenging for food and at times found themselves being snatched by hungry stingrays lying beneath the sand.

'We should be part of a school,' said the Juvenile Bluefin.

'Why? Didn't you see what happened to the mackerels the other day? They were all swimming in a school, which was why they were so easy to pick off. If we do the same then won't we become easy prey?' asked one of his friends.

'No we won't. We will have safety in numbers. If we swim amongst a large school of bluefins then that will increase our individual chances of surviving an attack. If a shark attacked us now then almost certainly one or more of us will be killed and eaten, but in a large school there is a chance that we could all survive an attack.'

The Juvenile Bluefin's friends were not convinced, what they saw the other day with the school of mackerel convinced them that his idea was not a good one. As they were all thinking about this, a large school of bluefin tuna swam over them from above. They all looked up at the school, all swimming together in perfect unity. The Juvenile Bluefin tried to convince his friends again to join the school but they both refused, he therefore bid them farewell and swam up towards the large school of bluefins.

His friends looked up and watched him fall in line with the school.

'There must hundreds of them there.' One of his friends thought to himself. 'Many of them will soon be killed and eaten by predators like sharks. I hope he will not be one of them.'

Over the weeks, the Juvenile Bluefin found that there were other advantages to living within a school. He found that it was easier for him to obtain food as there were so many of them on the lookout for potential prey and it also gave him better social interaction with his own kind. Then, the day came when they would face an attack by predators. A group of sharks were swimming towards them, the school found themselves being attacked from all sides. The sharks charged in one at a time and then when more of them appeared they began to charge in greater numbers. Several bluefins fell victim to the sharks, for some, the last thing they saw was a large jaw full of sharp teeth heading straight towards their faces. Others felt themselves being dragged from behind until they were trapped within the jaws of the sharks. However, when the sharks had finished their feeding, the school did not look any smaller than it did before the sharks came and the Juvenile Bluefin had survived.

Several days later the juvenile bluefin saw one of his old friends again from before he joined the school. 'Why are you alone?' He asked his old friend.

'I'm afraid we were attacked yesterday by an orca. Our friend did not survive,' said his old friend.

'Why don't you join the school? You will be safer here, sharks attacked us the other day but because of our numbers I managed to survive.'

'No. I do not feel safe here and why should I risk my life to save others when I have my own life to worry about.' Replied his old friend and then swam away from the school.

The Juvenile Bluefin watched his old friend swim away as he kept himself in line with the school. He would never see him again.

* * *

When we band together and are willing to make sacrifices to help everyone equally, then we can all benefit from having the same chance for success.

43 - The Barn Swallow

A Young Barn Swallow was on his way towards Britain. He had been travelling for several weeks, seeking the safe haven of Britain where at this time of the year, food would be plentiful and predators would be few. His journey had taken him from Africa, across the Mediterranean Sea and into Europe. When the air cleared and he could see the unmistakable White Shores of Dover, his long journey was almost over. He turned and momentarily flew into the winds direction to gain altitude as he was nearing land. The Swallow flew straight towards the River Dour, his long journey had made him thirsty and he now needed to drink. He flew down towards the river and when he was close he slowed the speed of his flight and raised himself a little before lowering his body over the river's surface until he almost touched the water. He skimmed the water's surface with his pointed beak, scooping as much water as he could take before raising his flight again and flying to a nearby telegraph pole where he perched himself on the wire. Soon, more swallows would arrive and the skies of Britain would be filled with the arrival of these birds.

He spent his first few weeks in Britain feeding and resting, enjoying the warm weather and the abundance of food available to him. Flying insects filled the air making it easy for him to seize a moth or crane insect with his beak during flight.

After a month, the Barn Swallow had found himself a mate and they built a nest out of mud and plant fibres in the corner of a barn ceiling, where they successfully raised several chicks.

As the end of summer approached the Barn Swallow still remained in Britain despite many of his kind already leaving. They were starting their journeys back to Africa to avoid the cold harsh British Winter. He however, continued to enjoy the warm weather and the food that was available to him here. He also spent much time perched on telegraph poles and rooftops singing and feeding whenever he spotted a flying insect. He did not want to think about his imminent and arduous journey back south, the thought of it made him feel unhappy. He wanted to enjoy himself as much as he could for as long as he could.

Before long, winter had finally come and the atmosphere was noticeably colder. Food was now almost impossible to find and it was becoming more difficult to find a safe warm place to rest. The barn swallow finally decided to make his journey back to Africa. As his journey progressed though he did not find it any easier to find food. The weather continued to be cold no matter how far he travelled each day. The Barn Swallow worked even harder, flying longer and faster each day to cover more distance, but it was no use. He was still trapped within the cold winter of Europe and Africa was still a long distance away. He finally realised that he had started his journey too late and therefore found himself still within the lands of Europe during these cold winter months. Before long the Barn Swallow died of exposure and starvation.

* * *

Time can be a valuable asset to us all but if we do not spend it wisely then it can become a liability.

44 - The Emperor Penguins

It was late autumn in Antarctica, the vast land here was made up almost entirely of ice and snow as far as the eye could see. To look around, one would see endless amounts of ice and snow on flat land but then the shape of the land would be altered by icebergs and mountains of snow that appear at random places. The temperature was getting even colder than it already was each day and the entire continent was almost devoid of any life. Except for a colony of emperor penguins, their distinct appearances made them stand out in the snow. The long thin black beaks with the orange stripe on the sides and black plumage of their faces, backs and wings coupled with the white plumage of their bellies going up to their slightly yellow coloured throats with the yellow and white colour plumage on the side of their necks.

The colony consisted of several thousand individuals and it was their breeding season now. They had courted and mated, and now the females were laying their eggs. After laying their eggs, the females then carefully passed the egg to the males, being careful not to let the egg touch the cold icy floor for too long. The males then carefully hold the egg between their feet and cover it with their brooding pouches to incubate them. The females then set off to sea to feed, they would need to eat enough now to provide food for their eventual offspring later. They walk with short strides, their bodies tilting slightly from left to right with each step until they find a break in the ice where they then take a deep breath before jumping into the water, head first. They swim into deep water almost like they are gliding with their wings outstretched, leaving behind white trails of bubbles that slowly fade into transparency.

The male penguins meanwhile huddle together for warmth, forming a large circle of bodies, their backs facing outwards and heads lowered to avoid the winds. Each held the egg between their feet carefully as they took turns to stand near the warm centre of the huddle. They will stay this way for two months and as the days go by, each day will provide less daylight than the last until eventually the males will stand in complete darkness and will not see daylight again for several weeks.

The females by now have swum many miles away from their breeding site and are feeding frantically. They swim fast and constantly, snatching any fish, krill or squid with their beaks. As soon as they spot potential prey, they go straight towards it at full speed, swimming at speeds of up to six miles per hour. Turning and manoeuvring left and right in split seconds as they chase their prey. One female darted straight into a school of fish splitting their formation apart and isolating one of them. The fish tried to evade her by changing directions at random but she was persistent, the fish swam lower and then tried to suddenly swim higher to catch her by surprise. The female penguin though cut the distance between herself and the fish by keeping her distance before darting straight forward as the fish swam higher, catching it with her beak.

Back at the breeding site, the males continue their daily struggle. The days were now continuous darkness, with temperatures as low as minus fifty degrees and winds of up to ninety miles per hour. Their only comfort now is that the eggs have now hatched and they can now see their own children. One father saw the head of his son poke forward from beneath his pouch, the chick looked cold and hungry. He feeds him with a substance from his mouth despite being weak and hungry himself before gently shuffling forward in the huddle to move closer to the centre for warmth. The other penguins reluctantly moved aside for him, some moving themselves towards the outer perimeter of the huddle, keeping their heads down as they did so. All the males themselves were starving now, having not had any food for nearly two months they have lost over half their body weight. It would be a few more days before the females would return, only then will they be able to leave the breeding site and save themselves.

Meanwhile, the females were now returning. After two months at sea, their bellies were now full and they must return to their mates and take over the care of their offspring. They found a large break in the ice and began swimming towards the surface. They jumped out of the water and into the air before landing on the icy surface on their bellies. Some of them struggled to their feet as they made their way back to the breeding site, others found it quicker to continue sliding on their bellies. As the female penguins were all jumping out of the water, a large leopard seal had followed them to their landing area and clambered out of the water's edge. The leopard seal was not as fast and agile as the penguins but in their state of panic and rush to get away, one female found herself in the wrong place at the wrong time. The leopard seal grabbed her by the left leg and began dragging her away. The captured female penguin kept completely still, fooling the leopard seal by playing dead. As the leopard seal dragged her limp body it stopped to catch its breath and let go of the penguin believing it was already dead, but then suddenly the penguin slid away before struggling to its feet and making her escape. The injured penguin was bleeding and walking with a limp now but still she persists and continues with her journey back to the breeding site, determined to see her mate again.

Back at the breeding site, some of the males have heard the first calls of the returning females. A few on the outer perimeter looked up into the distance and saw the small figures of the returning females slowly appearing. More of them began to look up towards the approaching females as they wait patiently with their offspring. As the females approach, their calls became louder and the males began to disperse from their huddle. Both the males and females began calling to their mates anxiously. As the calls continued, some penguins had found their mate and the pass over of the offspring from male to female began. Over the next few hours the breeding site swelled in numbers and there were penguins that could be seen in pairs everywhere.

As the day ended, most of the males had now left for the sea to feed after passing over the care of their offspring to the female. One male though was still there, he was blind in one eye and kept calling out for his mate but his calls were unanswered. In the last few hours he had witnessed several other males whose calls went unanswered and they had to abandon their chicks in order to save themselves from starvation. The abandoned chicks soon died. He knew that it wouldn't be long before he would have to contemplate doing the same; the thought of it aggrieved him. After calling out for another hour, the lone male then made the decision to leave and abandon his son to his fate before he too would die.

The injured female had finally made it back to the breeding site, the wound to her left leg was still there and she was still walking with a limp. When she reached the breeding site, she found that all the males had gone, her mate was nowhere in sight. She continued to look around but found only other females feeding their children and dead penguin chicks lying on the floor. Then suddenly, she found a lone chick, abandoned, cold and calling out in desperation. She approached him and took him as her own. When she looked down, she knew that he was hungry and began feeding him by regurgitation the food she had eaten during her time at sea.

Twenty-four days later the males had returned and again the breeding site became more crowded in numbers. The male who was blind in one eye and abandoned his chick was walking around the breeding site in search of a new mate but instead found something more familiar. He saw a female penguin caring for a chick whom he recognised, it was his own son but the female penguin was not his mate. He slowly approached them.

'Who are you? And why are you with my son?' asked the male.

'I returned to this site in search of my mate and child but I never found them. Instead I only found this child,' said the female.

'Why did you save him?'

'I had given birth and left my mate and child to hunt in the dangerous seas for two months. Then I survived an attack by a leopard seal. I could not let all of that be for nothing so I had to save this child otherwise my work would have been in vain.'

'Thank you. Thank you for saving my child. Because of your great deed, I have not completely failed as a father to my son.'

The male penguin who was blind in one eye chose the female as his new mate and together they raised his offspring.

* * *

To accept and love someone despite having no obligation to do such a thing for someone who is not even your own is a virtue of great significance that reaches out to others and beyond.

45 - Yellow Leaves

Autumn was fast approaching, the temperature was significantly cooler and there was a soft breeze that blew across the street. The branches on the trees all slowly flowed and stretched towards the direction that the wind blew and then returned to their original position. The trees all stood on the edge of the wide pavements on both sides of a long straight road, in front of various establishments. The streets were almost empty of people at this time and the ground was beginning to be covered with yellow leaves, there were few leaves that covered the middle of the road but there were many that fell to the side, reaching high enough to be level with the edge of the pavement. The pavements were covered more greatly, like the roads the edges which were closer to the trees had many more leaves covering them. Further in, leaves were spread all over the pavements randomly, some places they were evenly spread and in some areas they formed a pattern marked out by leaves piled onto one another, forming what looked like small empty lakes surrounded by land made up of yellow debris. The leaves moved as the wind blew again, rolling and floating, first in one direction and then suddenly moving in a different direction. The roads suddenly began to look more crowded in the centre like yellow insects crawling towards each other.

The trees were starting to look bare, slowly being stripped away of their natural green vegetation. One tree though had lost most of its leaves already and there were just two remaining, both hanging near the tip under a single branch, next to one another. They were both a light yellow colour.

'It seems like a despairing time, all of us having to leave our natural home. Soon we will join everyone else down there, strewn across the ground. Not knowing where we might land,' said the first leaf as she looked around.

'It's not all bad, if you look carefully the lands around us look even more beautiful than it used to and we get to be a part of it. That is the beauty of autumn,' said the second leaf.

The first leaf smiled as she looked at the second leaf. 'That's true but I am not as beautiful as the other leaves. I am much older for this is not the first autumn I am about to face. I am not as young as I use to be.'

'Really? I did not know that a leaf could survive more than one autumn or winter. How old are you?' asked the second leaf.

The first leaf laughed and shied away from the question. 'Age is of no significance now and neither you nor I need to know.'

'You say you're not as young as you use to be but you still look the same as you did when I first saw you but just in a different colour. There is no part of you that has withered, you are as smooth as you were when I looked upon you in the summer.'

The wind began to blow again for a few seconds and for a moment the two leaves were closer together and touched.

'It is only a matter of time now before you or I shall fall and for the first time in a while we will no longer be together. It saddens me to know that I may never see you again,' said the second leaf.

'We will see each again, although we may fall to the ground, it does not necessarily mean we will not fall together or that we will not land in the same place,' said the first leaf. A few seconds later the wind blew again and stronger this time.

The two leaves were pushed together by the strong wind and then when it suddenly stopped, the two fell quickly back into place but the first leaf's stem suddenly broke and it began to fall. She fell slowly and veered to her left and then slowly to her right as she fell the ground. The second leaf watched in despair as she left her place by his side, her image slowly getting smaller and smaller until eventually she landed on the ground below. Her image blending in with the rest of their kind and he could barely see her. He was alone now, a single leaf hanging under a branch of a tree.

That night the wind continued to blow unrelentingly and the second leaf found himself being twisted and turned until eventually he too fell, the wind carried him a fair distance away from the tree before he landed on the ground. There was empty space before him in every direction for several feet until the piles of other leaves would appear and he was in the centre of this oval like shape of space. He thought of the first leaf and then fell asleep.

When the second leaf awoke the next morning he looked to his right and found the first leaf next to him. 'It's you?'

'The wind brought me here during the night. It is good to see you again,' said the first leaf.

The second leaf smiled. 'Remember what I said about the beauty of autumn? Its beauty and elegance can take many forms and this is one of them.'

The two of them talked for a while until they saw something in the distance. Two people were approaching, one of them was significantly larger than the other and was holding the smaller one's hand as she jumped and hopped as they both walked. When they were both close enough the young child shook off her mother's hand and ran towards the two leaves. She looked at them both and smiled and laughed, feeling happy and excited as she saw in her child's mind how elegant and lovely they looked. She reached down and picked up the first leaf and then waved her around in the air before running back to her mother.

A few hours a later another person came by. This time it was a man with a bag collecting leaves. He picked up the second leaf from the ground and placed him in the bag.

Later in the day, the man who had been collecting the leaves had put them on display during a class he was teaching. He expressed the importance of autumn as one of the four seasons and used the leaves he collected as a symbol of the coming season. He expressed the aesthetic value of autumn, how beautiful the leaves all looked and he asked his students if any of them ever played in a bed of autumn leaves, many raised their hands. He also stated that autumn was also important because it is a sign of winter coming and nature's way of telling us to be prepared for it, such as animals who use the fallen leaves like the ones he displayed to build their winter homes. Then he explained the spiritual meaning of autumn, explaining that it signifies the balance between night and day and a sign of neutrality and peace between good and evil.

When the class ended he decided to take one of the leaves home with him for his daughter whom he knew admired the look of autumn leaves. He picked one out at random and then went home. When he got home he showed the leaf to his daughter but she already had one in her hand.

'Which one do you prefer then?' The man asked his daughter.

'I like both the same. They are both very beautiful and I want to keep both of them father.' replied his daughter.

The man looked and smiled at his daughter. 'Why don't I make these leaves last longer for you so then you can keep them for longer?' He asked.

His daughter nodded enthusiastically.

The man then took both leaves and had them preserved in a special solution for a few days. When he was happy that they felt soft and pliable he then dried them out and placed them in a glass picture frame before giving it to his daughter who was thrilled with the gift.

'I am glad to be able to see you again,' said the first leaf.

'We are together again. It seems that the beauty of the autumn has kept us together.' replied the second leaf.

The two yellow leaves stayed together, preserved in the picture frame for many years. They were very happy.

* * *

What was beautiful in the past will still be beautiful in the future as long as everyone wants it to be.